Dear Readers,

It's even more fun the second time around! You'll want to own all four of these sizzling new romances. So stack 'em up, curl up in a comfortable chair, and indulge!

Kate Holmes, multipublished as Anne Avery, used to work for the state department in South America—hence the romantic Rio de Janiero setting for her first Bouquet romance, **Amethyst and Gold.** A shy young teacher and writer, Melisande visits Rio to do research, never dreaming that she will be swept into the sensual rhythms of Carnavale . . . and into the arms of a handsome tycoon!

Veteran author Ann Josephson (you may know her as Sara Jarrod) has created one of the most appealing romantic heroes we've ever encountered in Brand Carendon—lawyer, athlete, and father of an eleven-year-old son he never knew he had . . . until first love Dani Murdock finds her way back into his life. Brand vows to make up for lost time . . . and to find **Enduring Love.**

Newcomer Debra Dawn Thomas takes her readers into the exotic, breathtakingly exciting world of Spanish bullfighting in her debut novel, **Wrap Me In Scarlet.** Sensible Stephanie Madison, a journalist looking for a story, finds much more in the arms of "El Peligro"—"The Dangerous One"—in a world of intoxicating adventure . . . and passion!

Suzanne Barrett, herself a facility engineer, gives her exciting profession to feisty heroine Karin Williams. She's sent to England to prove her skill alongside Rowan Marsden—a man who'd vowed never to work with a woman again. But Karin's talent, wits, and beauty combine to provide success in a business partnership and, ultimately, in **Taming Rowan.**

Decorate your life with a Bouquet on every table . . . four fresh new ones every month!

The Editors

NOT JUST A SAMBA

He wrapped his arms around her tightly, and drew her back into the dance. They might have been welded together as the rhythm of the music changed . . .

"You can't dance the samba like this!" Melisande said. It was hard to breathe, he was holding her so tight.

"I can." He swung her about as the music grew wilder, fiercer, more primitively erotic. Her blood was running hot and sweet and hungry with a desire so sharp and aching that it pierced her like a sword. Until the drums thundered to a halt that left her ears ringing and her head spinning.

"Now what do you say?" Alex demanded, his lips brushing the shell of her ear. His hand slid up her spine, holding her as he bent her backward.

Melisande gasped and clasped her hands around his neck. She couldn't have stopped herself if she'd wanted to . . .

"Melisande . . ." Her name came in a trembling whisper. His hand lifted to caress her face, then slid behind her neck as his thumb gently forced her chin up. Slowly, achingly slowly, his lips came down to meet hers with a driving, hungry force that obliterated the world around them . . .

AMETHYST AND GOLD

KATE HOLMES

Zebra Books
Kensington Publishing Corp.

http://www.zebrabooks.com

ZEBRA BOOKS are published by

Kensington Publishing Corp.
850 Third Avenue
New York, NY 10022

First Printing: August, 1999
10 9 8 7 6 5 4 3 2 1

Printed in the United States of America

ONE

She bodysurfed in on the foaming wave, then rose and raced up the beach before the next wave could catch her and sweep her off her feet.

The brisk tingling from the South Atlantic waters made her welcome the warm, moist heat of the beach. Glistening droplets of water slid off her skin, shimmering on the brilliant green of her body-hugging, high-cut maillot.

Though she couldn't see them clearly, she knew the men near her were studying her unabashedly. If she'd been wearing her contact lenses, she would have taken advantage of her right to return the favor in equal measure. The thought made her smile in good-humored recognition of the mutual girl-and boy-watching that was one of the chief entertainments of Ipanema beach.

The frank stares that slid from her face to her small, firm breasts, the nipples raised by the cold water, glided down her slender hips and long legs, and ended with a careful inspection of her ankles would have embarrassed her in New York. Here she was as free to admire the lithe, masculine bodies surrounding her as these men were to enjoy the sight of the beautiful Cariocas in their skimpy tangas.

Melisande Merrick, she thought to herself wryly, *two days in Rio and you're going native!*

She grinned, debated going back to where she'd left her towel, glasses, and sandals, then decided to enjoy her morning's freedom a little while longer.

With a happy skip, she headed up the beach. Before her was the vast stretch of sand where Ipanema beach became Leblon beach, and Leblon ended in the green hills that rose abruptly at its far end almost a mile away. Not too far behind her, she knew, was Arpoador beach and the Ponta do Arpoador, the point which divided Ipanema from the even longer curve of Copacabana beach.

The Atlantic water, warmed by currents coming from Africa and across the equator, came rushing up the sand after her, curling around her feet with a hiss of foam before sliding back to meet the next wave coming in.

As she walked, Melisande looked about her with the same sense of delight and wonder that had struck her the day before when she'd arrived. Without her glasses or contact lenses, she couldn't perceive anything clearly, and people only a few hundred feet away were only an animated mass of color without any distinguishing characteristics. But even her myopia couldn't dull the brilliance of the impressionistic picture before her. From the white sand at her feet to the intensely blue sky above her, the world was painted in vivid colors. The contrast with the dull browns and grays of the New York she'd left only two days before made her enjoyment all the sweeter.

Melisande gave another skip as she thought of those last, busy days in New York. The faculty meeting she'd attended had been noteworthy for a bitter wrangle about university policy. Absolutely nothing of scholarly or intellectual interest had been said at that meeting, or at ninety percent of the faculty meetings she'd had to attend during her three years as associate professor in the history department of one of New York's leading universities.

As she'd rushed about setting her affairs in order or making last-minute purchases, Melisande had been aware of the almost hostile tension that was so much a part of life in New York. The crowded streets, piled with dirty, gray snow, had seemed even noisier and more crowded than ever. By the time she'd finally collapsed in her seat on the plane, Melisande was heartily sick of the city that had been her home for most of her life.

Now here she was, walking along Ipanema beach in Rio de Janeiro, warmed by the hot, tropic sun of midsummer and contemplating four delicious months of doing what she liked to do best: historical research. Tomorrow she'd move into the apartment belonging to the Brazilian professor who would be using her apartment in New York. The research assistant a colleague had helped her hire had told her the day before that mounds of information already awaited her.

Most wonderful of all, she was going to be able to finish her book. That unexpected research grant had been a gift from the heavens. With the money from the grant she could complete the last phase of research here in Brazil. Who was she to complain if that research got her out of New York in the middle of winter and onto one of the world's most famous beaches in a city whose name was synonymous with romance?

Suddenly eager to get on with her work, Melisande turned and jogged back to where she'd left her things. When she spotted the hot-dog stand across from her hotel, she began looking for the set of volleyball stakes that had been her third point of reference. She'd learned long ago to compensate for her myopia with such tricks.

Orienting herself by the hotel, hot-dog stand, and volleyball stakes, Melisande headed to the spot where she'd left her possessions. Nothing. She checked her reference points again. She was where she was supposed to be. Her things were gone.

Perhaps she'd left them a little closer to the street. The tide might have gone out a bit, making her think she'd left her belongings nearer to the waterline than they really were.

Still nothing.

Worried now, Melisande began quartering back and forth like a hunting dog on the scent of a squirrel. She squinted, trying to force her eyes to see clearly without her glasses. All in vain.

Panic stabbed at her. It was one thing to walk along a beach without being able to see clearly. It was quite another to contemplate crossing six lanes of rushing traffic while half-blind.

"Excuse me, did you see a towel and a pair of glasses and sandals here?"

Melisande was embarrassed by the nervous tension she could hear in her voice. The older woman she'd approached glared at her in incomprehension and walked off.

"Excuse me."

Melisande cursed herself for not having made the time to take some lessons in Portuguese, the language of Brazil. The young man lying on a towel grinned up at her in friendly admiration, but his shrug said clearly he didn't understand what she was saying.

Two more attempts to ask people nearby were equally fruitless. Melisande found herself trembling. The six lanes of traffic might as well be a hundred. Without her glasses she couldn't cross the road to the hotel by herself.

In desperation, she approached a tall man coming up toward the street from the water's edge. "Excuse me."

"May I help you?"

"You speak English!" Though she couldn't distinguish his features clearly, Melisande was instantly aware of a sense of confident power that seemed to radiate from the man before her.

"Yes. What can I do to help you?" His voice was deep and very pleasant.

"I can't find my towel and things," said Melisande hesitantly, squinting up at him. She had an impression of strong features, all sharp lines and planes. Even without her glasses she could tell he was tall and powerfully built, with dark hair and dark eyes.

"Do I pass inspection?"

The note of amusement in his voice made Melisande blink, then blush and back off a few inches. "I'm sorry. I didn't mean to be rude, but I can't see well without my glasses."

"And they were with your towel."

"That's right. I thought I left it over there"—she

gave a vague wave toward where her things had been—"but I can't find it, and nobody speaks English so I can't ask if they've seen it."

"Why don't you show me where you think you left it, and we can start from there."

The man took her arm. His touch was unexpectedly warm and comfortingly protective. As she led him back to where she thought she'd left her towel, Melisande glanced up at him again. He was several inches taller than she was. She wished she could see his features more clearly.

"It should be somewhere around here. I tried to put it where I could find it again." She explained her points of reference to him.

Slowly the man pivoted on his heel, trying to spot an abandoned towel somewhere on the stretch of beach around them.

"I don't see any towel that's not occupied around here," he said at last. "I'll go ask if anyone has seen anything."

Her towel almost forgotten, Melisande watched him approach some of the people near them. Even without her glasses she could see that he moved with a powerful grace surprising in someone so large.

"I'm afraid your things have probably been stolen," he said when he came back. "The woman over there says she seems to remember a young boy picking up a towel around here, but she's not sure."

"My glasses!"

"Don't you have another pair?"

"Yes, but why would someone want to steal my glasses? Or a pair of cheap rubber sandals?"

Melisande could hear her voice tightening and

rising, but couldn't prevent it. The calm she'd felt with this stranger disappeared with the returning worry about crossing six lanes of heavy traffic to return to her hotel.

"This is a poor country, I'm afraid. Even the little a thief would get for your things is more than he had before he stole them. I'm sorry you should have this happen to you on your vacation, but it could have been a lot worse, you know."

Ignoring the comforting sympathy he was offering her, Melisande turned her head toward the busy avenue that fronted the beach. Even from this distance she could hear the roar of the passing cars. Fighting down a growing panic, she tried to assume an expression of calm. She didn't want to make a fool of herself in front of a stranger.

"Yes, you're right. Thank you so much for trying to help me."

Melisande couldn't take her eyes from the traffic she could barely discern. She swallowed painfully. Somehow she was going to have to cross that street. She didn't notice the stranger follow the direction of her gaze.

"That's it," he said, so softly she almost didn't hear him. "You're afraid to cross the street, aren't you?"

This time his words brought her around to face him.

"It's just that there are so many cars coming so fast, and I can't see them very well—until it's too late."

Her face, she knew, was slowly turning red with embarrassment.

"I didn't mean to make fun of you. Come on, I'll escort you across."

Again his hand was on her arm, warm and comforting.

"Oh, would you? Thank you! My hotel's the Praia Ipanema, right in front of us." Melisande smiled up at him in relief.

Her relief disappeared, however, when she tried to step onto the broad, black-and-white walkway that ran along the beach, dividing it from the broad avenue in front of them.

"Oh! It's hot!" she cried, jumping back onto the sand.

"I didn't think of that!" The stranger's laugh was delightfully deep. "Well, there's an easy solution to that problem, too!"

Before she could react, Melisande found herself swept off her feet and into a pair of strong arms that held her effortlessly against a broad chest. Startled, she wrapped her arms around his neck.

"You can't carry me!"

"Can you think of a better way to cross hot pavement when you don't have any shoes?"

"But you'll hurt yourself!"

"Not with a tiny thing like you." He laughed again. "Now don't distract me."

He turned slightly to gauge the oncoming traffic. Confused, Melisande looked over her shoulder. It needed only a glance to see what appeared to be hundreds of homicidal, metal behemoths bearing down on them at top speed. With a gasp of fright, she wrapped her arms even tighter around the stranger's neck and buried her face against his shoulder.

At least, she thought wildly as he stepped off the

curb into traffic, *if I'm going to die I'll die in the arms of a handsome man.* The light blue fabric of his shirt was smooth against her cheek. The musky scent of his aftershave, coupled with a vague, masculine smell that was part of the man himself, tantalized her.

Despite her concern that she was too heavy for him, the stranger carried her easily. He crossed the first three lanes of traffic without perceptible effort, his movements as smooth and powerful as they had seemed on the beach.

One car, roaring past them in the lane they had just crossed, made Melisande flinch. The stranger's sole reaction was to hold her even more closely against him.

The slight, protective gesture only served to increase what was becoming, for Melisande, an oddly intense awareness of the man who held her. Crushed against his chest and with her head buried in his shoulder, she could see nothing of his face. Her field of vision was limited to his shirt, the strong column of his throat, and the line of his jaw above it.

Even through his clothing she could feel the heat of his body against hers. The thought made her blush as she realized, for the first time since meeting him, that she was wearing only a bathing suit.

With the thought came awareness of the feel of his arms against her back and the soft flesh of the backs of her thighs. The awareness brought a flood of crimson to her cheeks. Thank heavens his need to concentrate on the traffic prevented him from looking at her right then.

He paused briefly on the barrier that divided the opposing directions of traffic, then darted across the remaining three lanes to the safety of the sidewalk in front of the hotel.

"Now that wasn't so bad, was it?"

Though he spoke in a joking tone, Melisande thought that carrying her must have been more difficult for him than she'd thought. She could feel his chest rising and falling in a oddly ragged rhythm, and the pulse at the base of his throat was beating much faster than before.

"Not at all."

Melisande found herself struggling to suppress a sudden, insane wish that the stranger wouldn't put her down.

"Service to your door. 'We deliver' is our motto."

Melisande giggled, then twisted in his arms to look in his face. He made no effort to put her on her feet. She thought he winked at her, but without her glasses she couldn't be sure.

Aware that she was starting to squint again in her effort to see more clearly, Melisande blushed and looked away, uncertain of what to say.

On the few occasions when she'd found herself in public without her glasses or contact lenses, she had tended to withdraw into herself not being able to see was simply too disquieting for her to face blurry-faced people calmly. Now, with the added confusion of finding herself in the arms of a stranger, Melisande was even more at a loss.

The stranger seemed not to notice her confusion, but continued, "There's a fee for the service, however."

Melisande thought she detected a teasing note in his voice. "What's the fee?"

"You have to let me buy you a cup of coffee."

"Coffee? On a hot day like this?"

"Fruit juice then. Brazil has some of the finest fresh fruits in the world."

He *was* teasing her.

"And if I don't agree?" she demanded with unaccustomed boldness.

"I'll take you back across the street and abandon you."

To accompany the threat, the stranger whirled about, still holding her closely, and moved toward the curb.

"No, no," protested Melisande, unable to restrain her laughter but clutching his neck nonetheless. "I'll have coffee *and* juice. Just don't take me back across the street!"

"Good."

The stranger carried her back into the shade of the hotel entrance. Melisande, looking up into his face, thought his eyes were glittering rather strangely as he gazed down at her.

"The fee for putting you down, however, is non-negotiable."

Before she could ask what he meant, Melisande found her lips caught in a kiss that began gently, but almost instantly turned into something far more demanding. Scarcely aware of what she was doing, she wrapped her arms even more tightly about his neck, drawing them closer together.

She didn't know how long the kiss lasted. It was a wave of cold air, released from the air-conditioned hotel lobby by someone going out the door, that brought her to her senses with a gasp.

Slowly, almost reluctantly, the stranger raised his

head. Once again his chest was rising and falling in a rapid, uneven rhythm.

"I'd carry you across anytime if that's the fee I can collect." His voice was suddenly rough, a little ragged on the edges.

Gently he lowered her to her feet. Disoriented by the kiss and her reaction to it, Melisande swayed for a moment against him. She was grateful for his hand supporting her until she could stand alone, but she was incapable of saying so. Her voice seemed trapped in her throat.

"Why don't you go on up and change?" he suggested. "I'll explain to the management that your towel has been stolen, then wait for you in the lobby. Is that OK?"

"Tell them I'll pay for the towel," said Melisande. She'd forgotten the theft. She tried not to think about the expression that must be on the doorman's face after their little exhibition. At least she was in Rio, where romance was expected!

While the stranger dealt with the hotel management, Melisande reclaimed her room key and went up to change, glad she'd followed the hotel's advice and left the key at the desk. From what she'd heard, a thief who found a room key usually went directly to the room and stole everything valuable before the hotel guest involved realized the key had been taken, let alone their other possessions.

A quick shower washed off the sand and salt. There was no time to dry her thick, shoulder-length brown hair, so she quickly tied it up in its usual knot at the top of her head. It was a relief to put her contact lenses in.

She pulled a simple cotton sundress out of the

closet, then paused. It was much too plain. She returned it to its hanger and pulled out a full-skirted, white piqué sundress covered in appliqués of brilliantly colored tropical flowers. The dress had been a special purchase for her trip. This would be the first time she would wear it. White, high-heeled sandals, a slight brush of eyeshadow to highlight the green of her eyes, and a touch of mascara to darken her already long, thick lashes completed her preparations.

As she rode down in the elevator, Melisande realized suddenly that she didn't really know what the stranger looked like, or even what his name was. Now that she could see clearly, would she be able to recognize him without having to go up to every blue-shirted man in the lobby?

Her fears were unfounded. She still didn't know his name, but she could have spotted him in a far more crowded place.

It wasn't that he was tall, because several other men passing through the busy lobby were of equal height. And while he was definitely good-looking in a very masculine way, she could see at least two others who could be considered more handsome.

It was, she decided, the air of power and energy that clung to him, even in the busy, crowded, and impersonal hotel lobby. He attracted attention without trying.

He spotted her when she was halfway across the lobby. Now that she had her contacts in, she could tell, even at this distance, that he approved of her appearance.

"Twenty minutes," he said with a smile as she

came up to him, "that must be some kind of a record."

"I didn't want to keep my rescuer waiting. Especially since I still haven't said thank you properly."

For the first time Melisande was able to truly see what he looked like. Her impressions of a face shaped by hard lines had not been mistaken. There was nothing soft about the man before her. Only his dark brown eyes, deeply set in their sockets, were gentle. Right now they were alight with a warm approval that was singularly disturbing.

"Since you're here to pay the second half of your fee, I consider it more than sufficient thanks." The smile that softened his lips was warm and, oh, so tempting.

"I realized as I went up to my room that I don't even know your name, and you don't know mine." Melisande felt suddenly shy. She extended her hand hesitantly. "I am Melisande Merrick."

"Melisande," he said, as though he were rolling her name on his tongue, savoring it. He took her hand in his. "It is a name that becomes you. Mine's Alex Robeson."

"I'm grateful for your help, Mr. Robeson."

"Alex, please. I couldn't possibly take a woman for coffee if she insisted on using formalities."

The little sidewalk café to which he took her was on a quiet side street. Neatly bordered by a potted flowering hedge and containing perhaps a dozen small, white tables, it was almost empty after the morning rush. Alex guided her through the welter of tables and scattered chairs to a small table for two in the corner.

As he pulled out a chair for her, he gave a quick order in Portuguese to an approaching waiter.

"I have taken the liberty of ordering a fruit juice for you, since you didn't seem too attracted to the idea of coffee."

"That's fine, thank you." Melisande ducked her head. There was something in his gaze that disturbed, yet attracted, her.

"How long are you going to be in Rio?" Alex asked.

"Four months." Melisande knew her answer was too curt to be polite, but she was confused by her unaccustomed response to this man.

"Four months? Isn't that rather a long time for a vacation?"

At the surprise in his voice, Melisande looked up.

"I'm not really a tourist," she explained. "I'm a professor of history. I got a grant to finish a book I've been working on for the past two years, so here I am."

"What kind of book? Brazilian history?"

"No, not really. It's about the women who immigrated to the New World from Europe over the last three hundred years. I wanted to be sure I included South America in the study, because there has been as much immigration here as there was to North America. The problem is, most books that have been written about the region have been written by men. And they haven't been interested in what the women went through to come here."

Melisande found herself relaxing under the combined influences of a familiar topic and Alex's obvious interest.

"I already spent some time in Argentina, Chile,

and Uruguay, some of the other countries that were strongly influenced by their immigrant population over the past couple of centuries. This grant allows me to finish my work here. I came to Rio because it used to be the capital of Brazil and a lot of the archives I need are here."

At this point the waiter interrupted them by delivering their order. Melisande took a sip of the thick, rich juice placed before her.

"Mmmm. This is delicious! What is it?"

"Cashew juice."

The smile on Alex's face softened his hard features, lending them an almost boyish attractiveness.

"I'm sorry. You said cashew? That's a nut."

"What you refer to as a cashew nut grows on the top of the cashew fruit. We use the fruit itself to make juice. Most visitors have never tried it before they come to Brazil. I'm glad you like it."

Melisande returned his smile, surprised and intrigued. Cashew juice?

"Tell me more about your book. You seem rather young to be a university professor."

"I'm twenty-five," Melisande replied without self-consciousness. She was accustomed to such questions. "My folks pushed me through school. I skipped a couple of grades along the way and got my bachelor's degree when I was nineteen. Then I did a combined master's and doctoral program, so I got my doctoral degree when I was twenty-two."

"Wasn't that rough, being a pretty young girl and having to spend all your time studying instead of having fun like everyone else?"

The real concern and interest in Alex's voice took the sting out of his question, but Melisande could feel the slight flush staining her cheeks. It *had* been rough, being younger than anyone else in her class, being forced to study when others her age were out playing.

She shrugged, brushing off the remembered sense of being different, of being apart from everyone else. "I got used to it. And I love my work. I've wanted to be a historian for as long as I can remember."

That, at least, was true. But it didn't say anything about the loneliness she sometimes felt working alone in echoing archives. Though she liked all sorts of people and enjoyed being with them, she'd never learned what every other young woman her age seemed to know—how to flirt, chase boys, date.

From the expression in his eyes, Melisande got the impression Alex was reading between some of her lines. She was grateful when he changed the direction of the conversation.

"How did you get interested in women immigrants?"

"From the work I did for my doctoral dissertation. I wrote about the Irish at the time of the potato famine during the last century. It was heartbreaking to read some of the journals and letters of women who had to uproot themselves and their families to follow their men. After I got my doctorate, I converted my dissertation into a book, *The Famine*. It was so much more interesting writing for the general public than for a scholarly audience that I decided to write another book."

Alex listened intently through her rather long explanation. Melisande would have found his interest appealing even if he hadn't been good-looking. Too many of the eligible men she'd met over the years had either been bored by her scholarly interests or intimidated by her academic achievements. Alex Robeson was neither. Under his intent, thoughtful gaze, she blossomed.

"Of course," she added, "without the academic grant I received, I couldn't hope to spend so much time here on research. But my university granted me leave, and here I am!"

"Are you planning to stay in your hotel for all that time?"

"Oh, no! I couldn't possibly afford it." Melisande laughed. "The academic world is like a little club. When I got the grant, I put the word out that I was seeking a Brazilian professor who would be in New York at the same time I'd be in Rio and who would be interested in swapping apartments. I move into his place tomorrow. It's right here in Ipanema, so I decided to treat myself to a nice hotel while I waited."

His smile was as warm as the breeze that lightly brushed across her skin. She blinked, startled by the thought, and hastily took another sip of her juice.

"Here I've been, rattling on about myself and not giving you a chance to say much of anything," she said lightly, "while I don't know any more about you than your name."

And that you're strong, that your arms feel good around me, and that you definitely know how to kiss, she thought.

Alex shifted in his chair and shrugged. Was it only her imagination that he seemed to withdraw from her slightly?

"Not much to tell. I'm a businessman involved in a variety of businesses."

"Where are you from?"

He looked startled. "Where am I from? From here, of course."

Melisande gave a little embarrassed laugh. "I'm sorry. You speak perfect English with an American accent. Since we met on the beach, I guess I assumed you were visiting, just like me."

Alex relaxed. "My father was Brazilian, my mother American. I grew up here, but studied in the States. Look," he added, glancing at his watch, "I hate to say this, but I'm afraid I have to get to work. I hadn't really expected my morning stroll to turn out so pleasantly, so I'm rather late." He smiled to soften the explanation.

She smiled back, stifling a pang of regret that he was leaving.

"Do you have the telephone number and address of this apartment you'll be staying in? I would like to call you once you're settled."

Melisande beamed, relief washing through her. She would see him again, after all. Quickly she dug a notepad and pen out of her purse and scribbled down the information.

"Here," she said, handing him the scrap of paper. "Why don't you give me your number, too," she added with unaccustomed boldness.

"I have to run," Alex said, taking the paper with her address on it but ignoring her suggestion. He put some bills on the table and stood up. "It's been a pleasure, Melisande Merrick."

Melisande rose with him, pushing down the stab of disappointment at his leaving. "Thank you for the juice . . . and thanks for rescuing me this morning," she said, smiling up at him.

"The pleasure, I assure you, was mine."

He bent his head slightly, and for a moment Melisande thought he was going to kiss her again. It seemed as though her heart skipped a beat at the thought. Then he straightened, his expression suddenly serious, and extended his hand.

"Good luck, Dr. Merrick."

He turned abruptly and strode out of the café and down the street, leaving Melisande gazing after him and wondering vaguely why a simple handshake should set her senses to tingling so.

TWO

Melisande moved into the apartment early the next morning. A taxi transported her and her suitcases the few blocks, and the porter helped her carry her things up. She was met at the door by the housekeeper, Senhora Amado.

When she'd first talked to the Brazilian professor, Melisande had been delighted to learn that this woman, who had worked for his family for years, would remain in the apartment. For four wonderful months Melisande wouldn't have to worry about housecleaning or cooking. The escape from such chores was like frosting on the cake of her stay in Rio.

It didn't take long, however, for her to realize she was going to have to make the effort to learn some Portuguese, and quickly. Senhora Amado spoke no English, and though she could, with effort, understand Melisande's faltering Spanish, Melisande found it impossible to understand the woman's sibilant Carioca accent.

However frustrating communicating with the housekeeper was going to be, living in the apartment would be a delight. The living room had one whole wall of windows giving onto a balcony with a view of Ipanema beach and the ocean only partially blocked by surrounding buildings. There were two bedrooms. A third room was obviously the professor's study. The long library table which occupied the center of the room would be a perfect workplace for her.

Her research assistant, whom she'd asked to visit her that morning, was another delight. A petite, pretty young graduate student, Catalina Vargas spoke excellent English and had already procured information that would be important to Melisande's work. After several hours spent going over the material Catalina had brought her, then deciding which libraries and archives they would visit first, Melisande's head was spinning.

Though four months sounded like a long time, experience had taught her that it wouldn't be nearly enough. No matter how hard she worked or how much information she obtained, there was always more to learn, more to discover, more to do. Always. The key was to be organized and stay focused. And to have a little fun, too.

Her days quickly fell into a busy, productive schedule. Taking advantage of being only two blocks from Ipanema beach, she started each morning with an invigorating run on the sand. She was amused to find her custom of early morning exercise a commonplace in this body-conscious city where everyone—housewives, businessmen, and seniors, as well as young people—made a habit of a morning workout. Exercise classes, jogging, or, later in the day, volleyball made the beaches in Rio seem like an outdoor gym.

It wasn't hard, Melisande soon realized, to figure out who the northern tourists were. They started out white, turned a brilliant red, then converted to a dark brown color with peeling patches.

Because her clear, delicate skin burned easily, Melisande used sunblock lavishly and avoided the beach during the hottest part of the day, but it didn't take long for her New York winter white to disappear under a glowing golden tan. Unhealthy it might be, but there was something to be said for the effect. Even her hair was beginning to show reddish highlights that enhanced the green color of her eyes.

A quick shower back in the apartment after her run was followed by a light breakfast that always included some of the luscious tropical fruits available. Then Melisande began her day's work.

With Catalina serving as translator and chief digger in the wealth of the material stored in Rio's archives and libraries, Melisande spent her days with her nose buried in her rapidly growing pile of notes, commentary, quotes, and questions. Some nights she dined with other academics, and Catalina occasionally took her home to share a family meal, but most evenings Melisande spent making notes and arranging material so that it would be readily accessible when she was prepared to write the chapters she'd planned on Brazil.

When she wasn't working, she spent her time wandering through the neighborhoods around Ipanema—Leblon, Arpoador, Copacabana. The hundreds of shops carrying dazzling varieties of merchandise fascinated her, but she found herself even more drawn to the busy rush of humanity surrounding her.

Rio's unique combination of international sophistication and Brazilian charm and informality created a fascinating cultural kaleidoscope of artists, businessmen, tourists, and shop workers that engaged her writer's ear and eye.

Despite her absorption with the life around her, Melisande took care to remember that Rio was also a city of frequent, sometimes violent crime engendered by the stark disparities between the lives of the middle and upper classes and those of the hundreds of thousands of desperately poor people who eked out marginal existences in the shacks on the hillsides above Ipanema and in the vast *favelas* or shantytowns that surrounded and sometimes invaded the city. Though she remained alert to the possibility of robbery, she refused to let Rio's reputation for crime deter her from enjoying to the full the sights and sounds around her.

Melisande didn't like admitting it, even to herself, but as she walked she was always alert for the sight of a tall, black-haired man with warm brown eyes. At first she found it difficult to admit, even to herself, that she could be so anxious to find a chance-met stranger again, but she couldn't deny that she'd been disappointed when he hadn't called as he'd promised. Once she'd tried to call him herself, but had found that he wasn't listed in the local phone directory.

When she finally had to admit that he wasn't going to call her, Melisande tried to push all thought of Alex Robeson from her mind. It wasn't nearly so easy as she would have liked.

Several times she'd thought she'd spotted him walking along the beach, but when she'd put on her glasses, which she now carried in a little bag hung about her neck, she was always disappointed to discover it wasn't Alex. Sometimes she would be on the point of falling asleep, and, unbidden, the memory would come of how his arms had felt about her, of how his kiss had stirred her.

Fortunately, work and lots of it was the best antidote for a passing infatuation, and she had plenty. Whenever she found her thoughts wandering down a particularly unproductive path, all she had to do was dig out a difficult reference in Portuguese and get lost between her dictionary, her grammar book, and the text she was struggling to decipher.

After a few weeks of this hard but lonely schedule, however, she was more than delighted to accept an invitation to attend a cocktail party being given by one of the archivists with whom she'd been working. Marta Araujo was a charming, sophisticated person who was interested in Melisande's work. Since Marta's husband was an international businessman, Melisande was looking forward to meeting people outside her own academic field.

"A small group, dear, maybe thirty people," Marta said, beaming.

Melisand blinked. Thirty was small?

"Many of them will be about your age," Marta continued, "which is a good thing because you can't spend all your time shut up with these old books."

"Will they all speak Portuguese?" Melisande asked. Despite listening to the TV and radio and working with dictionaries and language books, she wasn't yet capable of carrying on a conversation in the soft, melodious language.

"No, no. Many of the guests are business friends of Jorge's, and most of them speak English. Don't you worry. You're a lovely young woman, and I'm sure you'll enjoy yourself."

Melisande smiled and said she was sure she would, yet she couldn't help wishing she could have gone to the party on the arm of a tall, dark-haired, brown-eyed man who kissed like an angel and whose arms felt like Heaven when they held her.

The phone sat on his desk, silent, utilitarian, and accusing.

Alex Robeson glared at it, resenting its presence. How many times had he picked up the receiver over the past few weeks, then returned it to its place without pressing a single number? A dozen? A hundred? More?

Every time he had intended to call Melisande Merrick, and every time he had hesitated, then retreated.

He wasn't sure whether it was the thought of her or his own cowardice that troubled him more. It wasn't like him to be distracted by the memory of a woman he'd met casually or to hesitate over following up on an equally casual promise to call.

Calling her would be so simple. He didn't even have to look up her address or phone number: Without intending to, he'd memorized both long ago.

That fact alone ought to be enough to warn him off. He hadn't memorized a woman's telephone number for years, and he didn't much like having done so now. Yet try as he might, he couldn't get Melisande Merrick out of his mind any more than he could forget her address and phone number. If he closed his eyes, he could see her as clearly as if she were still sitting across that café table from him, sipping her juice and smiling.

Smiling, not flirting. He couldn't remember the last time he'd met a young, beautiful, eligible woman who didn't try to flirt, deliberately and with calculated skill. It was one of the givens that came with the name he bore and the fortune he controlled. He'd learned that lesson early on, and he'd learned it well.

He glared at the phone, then deliberately turned his attention back to the papers on his desk.

Five minutes later, the words were still swimming on the page in front of him and the phone was still sitting there, reminding him of the call he'd promised to make . . . and hadn't.

With a sharp curse, Alex picked up the receiver and punched in the number Melisande had given him.

The phone rang once, twice. He was conscious of an unaccustomed tension as he waited for her to pick up, waited to hear her voice at the other end of the line. A third ring, then there was a response on the other line.

"Hello," said a soft voice he remembered all too well. "This is Dr. Merrick. I'm sorry I can't come to the phone right now, but if you'll leave your name and number . . ."

Alex let out a long, long sigh and slowly, very carefully, replaced the receiver in its cradle without saying a word.

As she dressed for the party, Melisande automatically started to put her hair up in the simple bun she usually wore, then paused. Slowly she released her hair, letting it fall about her face in heavy, silken waves that cast shadows into her eyes and the hollows of her high cheekbones. She paused, considering the effect on the young woman who gazed back at her from the mirror.

Slender figure set off by a simple white dress, skin golden from the Brazilian sun, dark hair softly glowing—Melisande wasn't sure she recognized the sensuous stranger facing her. She hesitated, then quickly gathered the unruly waves into their usual neat bun.

She paused to study the cooler, more familiar figure in the mirror. A bun was becoming, she told herself. It accented the delicate lines of her face, brought out the graceful curve of her throat. She wasn't beautiful, but she did think she qualified to be called "pretty." Her academic colleagues might not be impressed, but she was a woman, as well as a scholar, and "pretty" gave her that extra bit of confidence she needed at times like this.

When the taxi dropped her off at the address Marta Araujo had given her, Melisande was surprised to find herself in one of Rio's upper-class neighborhoods. The building looked exclusive and was obviously expensive.

When she stepped directly from the private elevator into a luxurious entranceway gleaming with indirect lighting and dozens of candles reflected in the antique, gold-framed mirrors on the walls, Melisande decided the penthouse lived up to its billing.

Before she could take stock of her surroundings, Marta Araujo came bustling up. For an instant, Melisande wondered if she'd come to the wrong place.

The efficient, professional archivist she knew had vanished. In her stead was an elegant woman dressed in red satin and sparkling with diamonds. The transformation was even more of a surprise than the luxurious surroundings.

"I'm so glad you came, my dear!" Marta exclaimed. "I was afraid you would change your mind at the last minute."

The woman was beaming with unfeigned pleasure at Melisande's presence. She turned to the short, distinguished-looking gentleman who had appeared at her side.

"Jorge, I'd like you to meet Dr. Merrick, the American historian I told you about. My husband Jorge, Melisande."

The man thus addressed shook Melisande's hand and smiled invitingly.

"I am delighted to meet you, Dr. Merrick," he said in heavily accented English. "Marta has been telling me all about your research. She has always maintained that not enough credit has been given to the women who shaped our country's history."

"It's true, Jorge. You know it," said Marta firmly. "I've told several people about your project, my dear," she added, turning back to Melisande. "You'll be besieged with questions tonight. I'm not the only one delighted that someone is making an effort to give the women some credit for a change."

"And we men, Dr. Merrick, are worried at what you might start," added Jorge Araujo with a teasing twinkle in his eye. "We gave women the vote, and now they want to take over the country. What will happen if they get included in the history books, too?" He rolled his eyes in mock dismay.

Melisande couldn't help laughing. "I might be nervous if I hadn't already read some of the excellent work your own scholars are doing in the field. But please, call me Melisande. Dr. Merrick sounds so formal and old."

"Two things you can't possibly be accused of being," Jorge replied gallantly. "I've never met a more beautiful history professor. But come," he added, ignoring her sudden blush, "let me introduce you to some of the people here. I will try to avoid the people Marta has already alerted to your work, but I'm afraid I won't manage to keep your presence quiet forever."

As he led her into the room, Melisande got her first clear view of the guests. She found a mix of elegantly dressed people of all ages seated and standing about the designer-decorated living room. French, English, and Spanish, as well as Portuguese, could be heard from the various conversational groups.

Jorge's warning, which Melisande had taken as nothing more than playful banter, proved to be accurate. Marta *had* told a fair number of people at the party about her project, and all of them were interested in knowing more about her work and how it was progressing. She soon found herself trying to keep track of a conversation which included questions from a serious, bespectacled professor, advice from an animated matron who seemed bent on telling Melisande *exactly* how to write her book, and odd scraps of comments and questions from several others who were also carrying on two or three other conversations at the same time.

Just as she was trying to decide if she could simply

walk away from the confusing welter of voices, a merry laugh from beside her caught her attention.

"René! Serious conversation at one of Marta's parties? For shame!"

A diminutive redhead claimed a spot at Melisande's elbow, laughing and shaking a mock-admonitory finger at the intense professor.

"And Catia, you must wait until Miss Merrick has a chance to start before you tell her how to finish!" This comment, accompanied by a mischievous wink at Melisande, was directed to the helpful matron.

Both of Melisande's companions laughed, and several others in the group grinned appreciatively at the animated redhead.

Her eyes twinkling, Melisande's rescuer drew her away from the cluster of people saying, "Marta sent me to rescue you! I'm Maria, Maria Sebastian, and I am to try to give you at least a few minutes' break before turning you loose again!"

"I'm very grateful!" said Melisande, laughing and following her to a quiet corner of the room. "I was beginning to lose track of everything! I had such an urge to say something naughty that I knew I'd be sorry for afterward!"

"I know *just* what you mean," said Maria, nodding an appreciative agreement. "René is a dear but *so* serious. And Catia! Well, if there's anything she doesn't know how to do better than anyone else, she hasn't yet found out what it is!

"Here," she continued, drawing Melisande aside. "Quiet, of a sort. So we can talk."

She grinned enchantingly and gave Melisande a conspiratorial wink. "To be honest, I had an ulterior motive for rescuing you—I want to hear all about your research, too! I've been anxious to meet you ever since Marta told me about your book. I'd love to know more about what you're doing."

Melisande couldn't help laughing at her companion's engaging frankness. "I'm really just getting started. You know, sorting through old records, which takes a lot of time, and getting to know what is available where. I did a lot of advance work before I came, but it will be a while before I have a good sense of what I'm working on here."

"I can't wait to read the book." The vivacious redhead's eyes were sparkling with enthusiasm. "But I'll bet you get tired of talking about your work when you spend all day doing it. Let me introduce you to my husband, instead, and maybe a few people who won't pester you as much as René and Catia."

She stood on tiptoe, trying to see over the people around her. "There he is, talking to Alex." She pointed, then added helpfully, "Alex Robeson. He's the tall, dark-haired man standing by that funny-looking modern sculpture Marta loves. My husband is the slender, blond-haired man next to Alex. He's a banker, but you'd never think it to look at him, would you?"

Melisande, slightly dazed by the rush of words and her unexpected, breath-tightening reaction to the name of a man she'd met only once, turned to look in the direction indicated. Taller than the people around him, including the man with whom he was talking, Alex Robeson seemed to exude a power, an almost tangible force of personality, which drew her attention even across the crowded room.

THREE

"I think Stephen's seen us," said Maria beside Melisande. "Yes! Here he comes with Alex!"

"Oh," said Melisande vaguely. Her gaze was glued on the tall figure following Stephen Sebastian through the crush of people.

"Alex!" Maria cried as the two men dodged the last knot of people to stand before them. "*Do* stop supporting Stephen's bad habit of talking business at parties. I want you to meet someone."

"I wasn't encouraging him, Maria," Alex protested. "He cornered me before I could get away!"

"I can believe that, but by now you should know better than to get caught. In any case, make your bow to Dr. Merrick. She's a professor of history and is going to write a book that will put all you men in your place."

As commanded, Alex turned toward Melisande. He'd been so intent on navigating through the crowd that Melisande knew he hadn't looked at her until that moment, yet despite his nonchalant air, she had the sense he'd stiffened at the mention of her name—whether from surprise or displeasure, she couldn't tell.

Certainly there was nothing but flattering pleasure in his eyes when he stopped before her, and his smile was warm enough to melt ice.

"We meet again," he said, drawing her hand into his.

Melisande gave a little gulp. She was suddenly and uncomfortably warm in the cool, air-conditioned room.

"Mr. Robeson," she said in acknowledgment, hoping no one would notice the slight tightening of her voice.

"Alex, remember?" The tension she thought she'd sensed a moment earlier had vanished—if it had ever been there at all. He smiled, his eyes teasing her with remembered intimacy. He released her hand with an air of reluctance.

"You've met? How in the world did you two meet before?" Maria demanded, agog with curiosity.

"Mr. Robeson, uh, Alex . . . ," Melisande started to say.

"Melisande . . . ," said Alex at the same time.

They both stopped, stared, then burst into laughter.

"Melisande was robbed on the beach in front of her hotel at Ipanema," said Alex at last. "I was able to help her."

Melisande hoped Maria never learned exactly *how* Alex had helped her. Unfortunately, Maria seemed to know Alex too well to let him get by with so simple an explanation.

"Oh, that's terrible!" she exclaimed. She paused, then unabashedly added, *"How* did you help her?"

Alex said nothing, but an arched eyebrow and twisting smile showed he knew that not answering would provoke the curious redhead.

"Alex helped me across the street," Melisande explained. She hoped her blush didn't show under the tan.

"The thieves took my glasses, and I can't see very well without them," she added when she realized Maria wasn't going to be content without an explanation.

"Well, at least Alex doesn't seem to have behaved the way he usually does," said Maria, still studying them. "If he had, you probably would have slapped him."

"Maria!"

The protest came from Maria's husband, Stephen. Until now, he'd been watching the interchange without speaking, but with a wide, appreciative grin on his face.

"Now, Stephen, I've known Alex longer than I've known you. Which is probably why I never considered marrying him," Maria added darkly, for Alex's benefit.

"You see," she said, turning toward Melisande, "Alex can be absolutely outrageous with women. He's rich and gorgeous, and women flock around him. It's gone to his head. He was much better behaved when we were children in school. Now that he's all grown up he sometimes gets completely out of hand."

Dimples showing, she grinned mischievously up at the man towering above her. Alex grinned down at her.

"You're a fine one to talk of outrageous behavior, Maria!" he said. "I've never lived down the time, in our teenage years, when you climbed up on a

chair to thump me on the head! Your lack of dignity
is appalling!"

"Hah! Stephen James! Defend your wife!" demanded the redhead, laughing.

"You don't need me to defend you, love," said
the blond man with a smile. He turned to Melisande.

"Dr. Merrick, you are not to take either one of
them seriously. They're both badly behaved and a
horrible influence on each other."

His smile was kind and welcoming. Melisande, despite her confusion at being involved in the teasing
argument, smiled in return.

"I hope you enjoy your stay here," Stephen continued in his quiet, pleasant voice. "Marta told us
about your work. I must say it sounds fascinating."
He leaned toward her and in an exaggerated whisper added, "My wife would kill me if I didn't say
that."

"Stephen James!" his wife protested indignantly.

"Now you know why I've stayed single all this
time, Stephen," Alex said with a straight face. "I
knew Maria would be a brutal wife, and I figured
if someone that little could be that tough, it would
be a disaster to try to handle any woman bigger
than she is!"

The redhead laughed, acknowledging a hit.

"Let's ignore these lunks, Melisande," she said,
drawing herself up in haughty dignity. "Besides being unspeakably rude, I can see that Stephen is dy-
ing to talk banking, and Alex is going to be
obnoxious and let him."

Melisande, who was all too uncomfortably aware
of Alex, was more than happy to follow her new

guide, but Alex's warm laughter held her like honey.

"When you start depicting me as being as boring as Stephen in one of his intense banking moods, I am truly warned, Maria." His words were for Maria, but his gaze was disconcertingly fixed on Melisande. "I suppose I shall have to reform my ways."

"Don't even try." Stephen heaved an exaggerated sigh. "My wife has won the fray once again. However, it at least allows me to finish my *very* interesting commentary on the new banking laws. A fascinating subject no matter what you all say!"

Melisande smiled as she shook hands with him, then turned to Alex Robeson, a hand outstretched. She hoped she looked calmer than she felt. A handshake was such a common gesture, yet just the thought of touching him had her heart racing.

"I'm glad to see you again, Alex," she said, and was pleased her voice sounded as steady as if she were discussing the weather with a stranger.

She left unspoken the question she burned to ask: *Will I ever see you again?*

Alex said nothing, but took her hand and smiled down at her. His hand was warm and strong, his touch as unsettling as she'd feared. Though she couldn't be sure, she thought she read a *Yes* in his dark eyes, and with that she had to be content.

"Ah, Melisande," Stephen added, "I don't know if you like sailing, but if you do, you're welcome on our little boat anytime. Or at least you are if it ever gets out of dry dock. We can give you a call the first time we go out."

As she accepted the invitation, Melisande could feel Alex Robeson's dark eyes watching her. The departure of the two men brought relief from the blush that heated her cheeks, yet as she watched them walk away, she couldn't tear her attention from the tall, broad-shouldered figure beside Stephen Sebastian.

Before either Melisande or Maria could say anything, Marta appeared beside them.

"Oh, good! I see Maria managed to rescue you from the crowd, Melisande. I told her she should. Besides being one of my favorite people, Maria is a marvelous dress designer, and I suggest that you visit her shop. Her styles would suit you very well."

Maria laughed and gave Marta a friendly kiss on the cheek. "You're the best press agent I have, Marta. And you took at least *some* of the words out of my mouth. I was going to invite you to stop by sometime," she added, turning to Melisande. "You're just the sort of person I like to dress up."

The three had a friendly laugh, then it was quickly settled that Melisande would call to arrange a special visit to the shop, which wasn't far from her borrowed apartment.

At that point someone came up to claim Marta. Melisande was introduced to two people she hadn't yet met, and the three separated with the flow of the party.

An hour later Melisande realized that Marta's small party of thirty had somehow grown to include at least twice that many. Though it seemed she'd talked to dozens of people she didn't know, Melisande could see several people she hadn't yet met.

Yet as she moved about, she couldn't help being aware of Alex Robeson as he mixed with the crowd, most of whom he seemed to know. Despite Melisande's hope that the movement of the guests would bring him around to her or, better yet, that he would seek her out, Alex didn't come anywhere near her. And, though she very much wanted to talk to him again, she couldn't bring herself to seek him out. When she finally decided it was time to leave, she couldn't spot him at all.

Aware of a vague sense of disappointment, Melisande went in search of her host and hostess.

"I'm so glad you came, dear," said Marta, hugging her. "Several people have said how delighted they were to meet you. Now, just let me go get Jorge and Alex. Jorge wanted to be sure to say good-bye, and Alex said I wasn't to let you leave without him, since he was taking you home. Don't move. I'll be right back."

With that, Marta disappeared, leaving Melisande too stunned to say anything, even if she'd had the chance.

Alex was taking her home? He hadn't said anything to her, hadn't even made an effort to talk to her after he'd gone off with Stephen Sebastian. And yet here he was leaving commands that she wasn't to leave until he said so!

She was inclined to refuse so high-handed an arrangement, but there was no denying she wanted to see him again. And wasn't his announcement that he was taking her home like a public admission that he wanted to see her again?

Before she could resolve her confusion, Marta reappeared with Jorge and Alex following in her wake.

As Melisande thanked her host for the evening, she caught Alex's eye. The combination of amusement and certainty she saw there forced her to look away quickly before she said something she'd regret. She'd wanted to see him again, but she wasn't interested in having him take her for granted. She still hadn't decided whether his high-handed approach was more annoying . . . or promising.

Alex stood holding the door open for her as she said her last thanks to the Araujos. He shook hands with Jorge and leaned down to kiss Marta on the cheek, then turned to her with what Melisande would describe as a proprietorial air. After all, they'd barely met. How could he assume he had any control over her?

"Do you want me to take you straight home, or would you like to stop for some coffee first?" he asked as the elevator door shut behind him.

"I'd like to go home, please," Melisande replied stiffly, fixedly watching the elevator lights as they registered the floors the car was passing. He seemed to fill the space around her with a sense of latent masculine power. The scent he wore—was it aftershave or cologne?—was subtle, almost imperceptible, and extremely unsettling. It made her think of kisses and his arm against her back and thighs, her breast pressed to his.

"The night's young yet," Alex said softly, "and this *is* Rio."

The suggestion carried in the way Alex spoke as much as in his words made Melisande shiver suddenly.

"Are you cold?"

He moved closer. Only a few inches, but it made Melisande wonder if the air had suddenly disappeared from the small space. "These luxury buildings do tend to be rather over air-conditioned at times."

"I'm tired," said Melisande, glad to take advantage of the excuse he offered. "It's been a hectic few weeks, and I have a lot of work to do tomorrow."

"You *are* dedicated, aren't you?"

The slightly mocking note she thought she heard irritated her. "Aren't you dedicated to whatever it is *you* do?"

"Yes, I'm dedicated to my work. But not to the exclusion of everything else."

Again Melisande thought she caught the subtle, provocative suggestion. She shrugged in irritation.

"You probably don't have four months in which to do double your usual amount of work."

Before Alex could respond they'd reached the ground floor. The doorman was holding the door of a Mercedes sports car open for them.

Maybe it was the fresh night air, or the still lively bustle of people on the street, but by the time Alex had settled behind the wheel, Melisande's irritation was rapidly being replaced by embarrassment at her behavior. Her response to his courteous gesture, she realized, was due more to her own uncertainty about her reaction to the man beside her than to any overt advances on his part.

It was easier to admit her error when all she could see of him were the sharp lines of his profile and the bulk of his big body highlighted by the subdued lights of the instruments.

"I'm sorry if I was rude," she said a little stiffly. "I didn't mean to be. I'm just not used to having anyone leave an order that I'm not supposed to leave a party until he says so."

Alex glanced over at her. Even in the dark Melisande could see he was surprised by her apology.

"I *am* grateful for the ride," she added. "People said I should be careful at night, so I appreciate your taking me home. And thank you, too, for the invitation for coffee, but I really do have a lot of work to do tomorrow."

To Melisande's surprise, Alex burst out laughing. "That should just about cover everything. And since apologies seem to be in order, I'm sorry if I seemed overbearing. I just didn't want you to be out on the street alone at this time of night."

Melisande sank back in her seat, smiling. Before she could reply, Alex continued, "I also wanted to have the chance to tell you that I did try to call you, but no one was home. Then business, work, you know . . ." His voice trailed off.

Perhaps the lame excuse troubled him as much as it embarrassed her.

He shrugged. "Since you can't spare the time for some coffee this evening, I would like to take you to lunch tomorrow."

The invitation surprised Melisande. For a moment she could only stare at him, uncertain how to respond. She wanted to say yes. But she wanted to say it so badly it was almost frightening. She wasn't sure that she should get involved with a man who had the power to attract her so easily. After all, she'd come to Rio to work, not indulge in romantic flings, no matter how tempting.

When she didn't answer immediately, Alex glanced over at her. In the dark, Melisande found it impossible to read his expression, but when he spoke, he sounded as if he were surprised by her hesitation.

"You do have to eat, you know," he said. "Wouldn't it be more pleasant to eat with someone than to eat alone?"

Melisande laughed softly. She was undoubtedly reading more into the invitation than it warranted. Perhaps she could blame it on the intimacy of being so close to him in the dark interior of the car. And he was right. It *would* be more enjoyable to share her meal than to eat alone, as she so often did when she was working.

"Thank you," she said at last. "I would enjoy having lunch with you."

"Good."

Before he could say more, Alex had pulled to a stop in front of her apartment building. She waited while he got out and came around to open her door for her.

As Alex helped her out, she glanced up into his face. Even with the brighter light cast by the streetlights and the glow from the surrounding buildings, his face was too shadowed for her to see his expression clearly.

"Shall I pick you up at, say, one o'clock?" he asked as he took her arm to escort her to the door. "I assume you'll be at home?"

"As it happens, I will. One o'clock would be fine."

Melisande smiled up at him. Standing in the well-lighted doorway, she could see that he was watching her intently.

"Good," he said, and smiled. "I'll pick a special place, just for you."

They rode up in the elevator in silence. Melisande had the sense his promise hung in the air between them, heavy with possibilities.

Alex took the keys from her hand and reached around her to unlock the door. Melisande's breathing quickened involuntarily as his arm brushed against her. Before she could move away, he'd straightened and turned back to her.

It seemed the most natural thing in the world for her to move into his arms, inevitable that she would be ready to receive his kisses. At first his touch was gentle, but as the kiss deepened Melisande could feel his rising urgency and found herself molding her body against his.

Though she'd had little experience with romance or kissing, and certainly had never before met a man like Alex Robeson, Melisande found it easy to respond to his skillful, practiced assault on her senses. Something within her, some innate, feminine knowledge, led her to meet his demands with urgent, sensual demands of her own.

When he finally released her, she had to steady herself against him for a moment, until she found the strength to stand on her own.

The shadows cast by the building lights couldn't hide the puzzled, wondering look that softened his features.

"It's still there," he said, so low Melisande wasn't even sure she heard him right. "Whatever it is, it's still there."

Abruptly Alex straightened, then shook his head

like a man coming out of a daze. He reached past her and wrenched open the door he'd unlocked.

"Good night, Melisande," was all he said before the elevator doors closed behind him.

FOUR

FOUR

Melisande spent the following morning working with Catalina, reviewing the information her research assistant had assembled and planning her work for the next few days. Once Catalina had left, she returned to studying some old books that Marta had obtained for her. As she worked, the sounds of the city coming through the window and of Senhora Amado's industrious vacuuming of the front room faded from her awareness.

It was the sound of fingers being snapped by her ear that finally brought her back to an awareness of her surroundings.

Startled, she looked up to find Alex Robeson watching her, his dark brown eyes alight with amusement. Without thinking, she pushed her glasses up her nose so she could see him better and caught her breath. Looking at him instead of the old books she'd been perusing was like drinking champagne after water.

"Are you always so wrapped up in your work?" he asked. "I knocked on the door and called your name, and you never budged. I was beginning to think it was going to take a firecracker to get your attention."

Melisande's smile changed to a rueful grin. "I'm

afraid I do tend to get absorbed in what I'm doing," she admitted. "Is it really one o'clock already? I asked Senhora Amado to tell me a few minutes before so I could be ready and not keep you waiting."

In the light sports jacket and open-collared shirt he looked, Melisande thought, exactly like every woman's most heated erotic fantasy. His vitality and animal magnetism were irresistible.

"I'm early," he said, "and I told her not to announce me. I want to suggest a change in our plans."

At his words Melisande was conscious of a stab of disappointment. She had been looking forward to their lunch together more than she'd thought. Before she could respond, he explained.

"I thought, since you've been working much too hard and you haven't been in Rio very long, you might like to take a few hours off. If you're game, we could take a bus so you can see some of the city, then take the cog railway and go up the Corcovado to see the statue of Christ. There is a pleasant outdoor restaurant at the top. We can have lunch there, and you will have a wonderful view of the city."

"I'd love to do that," she exclaimed. "If you'll just give me a few minutes I'll be ready."

The one-hundred-fifty-foot statue of Christ, arms outstretched, was one of Rio's most famous landmarks. It stood on top of the hill the Brazilians called the Corcovado, which meant the hunchback. The statue was reached either by car or by the more popular cog railway. From its base, the visitor had a panoramic view of Rio and its beautiful bay.

She'd been planning to go up Corcovado. It

would be infinitely more enjoyable to do it with Alex Robeson as her guide. And she *had* been working almost without letup, she assured herself. She deserved a little excitement for a change.

Leaving Alex to scan the books and stacks of documents and notes that littered her long work table, she retreated to the bedroom. She took a moment to exchange her reading glasses for contact lenses and a pair of sunglasses. After a quick glance in the mirror to assure herself that her makeup was neat and her light cotton skirt and top appropriate, she collected her purse and straw hat and returned to the study.

She found Alex casually slouched in a chair, dark hair falling over his brow. He was immersed in one of the old books. Melisande stopped in the doorway, watching him.

A sudden shyness overcame her. He was so completely masculine, so obviously in control of himself and those around him. She'd never met a man quite like him.

Then he glanced up at her and smiled. The smile softened the hard lines of his face, making him seem less intimidating and even more attractive. Her attack of shyness disappeared in the warmth that rose in her in response to his smile.

Though he didn't appear the type ever to have used so common a form of transportation as a bus, Melisande was surprised to find that Alex knew exactly which bus they had to take and where they could catch it.

She took a window seat. Alex sat down beside her. His arm brushed against hers and again he smiled at her. Though she knew the slight touch was unintentional, Melisande couldn't suppress the heat that rose in her. She didn't think she'd ever be able to suppress her intense physical awareness of him. She couldn't be in the same room without being intensely conscious of him.

So that he wouldn't guess the direction of her thoughts, she turned to look out the window. It was disconcerting always to be so susceptible to his slightest gesture or expression.

Fortunately, there was so much to see that she soon found herself caught up by the changing scenery and was thus able to relax a little.

From the tall, modern buildings of Ipanema they passed through neighborhoods with homes dating from the previous century, almost hidden behind the lush foliage and tall walls of their gardens. They passed parks, large and small, whose rich greenery provided a striking contrast to the tall office buildings around them. Occasionally Alex would point out a special landmark or tell her some of the history of the area.

The cog railway station was located in a quiet neighborhood where huge old trees hung over the streets, providing cool and welcome relief from the strong sun. Tucked away in a shady area between old houses, the station had more the air of a neighborhood gathering point than that of one of the city's major tourist stops. It certainly gave no hint that it was on the edge of one of Brazil's most famous national parks, the Tijuca National Park, of which the Corcovado was a part.

While Alex bought their tickets, Melisande studied the people around them—a young Brazilian couple obviously out for an adventure, some older tourists who looked German, an American couple with two small children who were racing about asking questions, and an unidentifiable mix of tourists and Brazilians sitting on the benches or standing in line for the next cars.

When the two red cars eventually came rattling down the hill and into the station, people bustled about to get in line while the departing passengers poured off, chattering and laughing.

As they settled into their seats, Melisande could barely repress the urge to laugh out loud from excitement and pleasure. The trip up the Corcovado was one she'd long looked forward to. Alex's presence made the trip special, indefinably out of the ordinary.

The little train pulled out with a jerk and a rumble. In just a few minutes they'd left the station and houses behind to enter a fairyland of greenery. Clusters of bamboo towered above them, the feathery leaves forming a canopy high over the tracks. Vines and plants obscured the bases of tall trees whose tops were lost above the lower vegetation. Butterflies flitted about, and Melisande was delighted to spot several species that were favored by collectors for their beauty, especially one particularly large butterfly whose wings glowed an iridescent blue in the light.

Alex laughingly protested Melisande's constant demands for names and information about the plants, birds, and butterflies they saw. "Hey, I'm a businessman, not a botanist!"

He studied the forest about them, his face relaxed, interested. He seemed suddenly younger, as though he'd left his cares at the bottom of the hill.

"This is so beautiful," she said softly, "it makes me wonder why anyone would spend time in an office when this is out here."

As they rose higher, the tracks began to run along the side of the hill, and they were provided with occasional glimpses, through the heavy greenery, of the city below them. Many of their fellow passengers moved about the car, trying to get photos from every possible angle, but Melisande was content to remain in her seat and enjoy the delights around her.

The station where they were to get off was located just below the peak of the hill, but the heavy vegetation and the angle of the slope obscured any view of the famous statue above them. They paused to let the other passengers go ahead of them, then started up the steps that led to the peak.

The statue soon towered above them, arms outstretched in blessing over the city below so that the body formed a huge cross. Melisande climbed the steps, her attention focused on the massive figure of Christ. As they came out of the protective trees, a strong breeze tugged at her skirt and threatened to steal her hat, but Alex caught it in time and returned it to her.

"It really is beautiful, isn't it?" asked Melisande, breathless with the grandeur of it all.

Alex stood for a moment, looking up, his hand lifted to shade his eyes; then he turned to smile at her. His eyes were alight with an excitement that matched her own.

"I've been here hundreds of times, and always I forget just how beautiful it is." He waved his hand in a gesture covering the city that they were just able to see below them. "Not just the statue, but the city and the land itself."

He grabbed her hand and headed up the stairs again. "Come on! The view at the top is even better."

His hand was large and strong and warm over hers, his enthusiasm contagious. Melisande scrambled to keep up with his eager steps, suddenly conscious of the easy way he moved, the subtle, controlled power that seemed so natural a part of him.

It wasn't just the stronger breeze at the top that took Melisande's breath away. The view wasn't just better, it was magnificent. Rio swept around the base of the Corcovado in a glittering white curve. Flamingo Bay and Copacabana, with Sugar Loaf rising gracefully between them, occupied the center of the view. At the far sides she could see the city center and Ipanema. Behind and immediately about her were the dark green tops of the forest that made up the national park.

The contrast between the sprawling, modern city and the ancient forest, which could only hint at what the land had been like before European settlers arrived, was reinforced by the changeless sweep of blue that made up Guanabara Bay.

Melisande had no idea how long she stood drinking in the splendor about her. Alex's gentle touch on her arm startled her into the realization that, for a moment, she'd forgotten his very existence. She glanced up at him in confusion, the smile of wonder still lighting her face.

"I'd begun to think you'd forgotten me," he said. The understanding Melisande could see in his eyes belied the reproach in his voice. He turned to look out over the city, then glanced back at her.

"It's good to be reminded every once in a while that Rio is truly something special." Alex reached out to draw Melisande to him while he turned back to the view of the city before him.

"It's also good to be reminded that there are many who don't share in that beauty," he said. "We tend to forget that, living in our comfortable homes on modern streets in nice neighborhoods with all the amenities."

Melisande glanced up at him, surprised at the sudden intensity in his voice. He'd pulled her to him, but despite the sudden stirring within her at his nearness she sensed that he'd reached out to her as another human being who could share his concern, rather than as a woman he wanted near him.

"Look there, and there."

Melisande looked to where he pointed, at crowded shanties spread like a blighting fungus across the rich green of steep hillsides bordering the gleaming, modern city.

"Those are the *favelas*, the shantytowns where hundreds of thousands of people exist without running water or decent sanitation, without even a decent roof over their heads. Families of six or eight people or more crowd together in one room with a dirt floor. There's never enough food, and there is little schooling for the children."

He released her, but Melisande was unable to move away, caught up in his unconscious fervor.

"There's no city in the world quite like Rio." His voice vibrated with passion, alive with his love for the land, inviting her to experience what he knew, what he felt. "She's beautiful and alive and bursting with energy, but she's also eaten at by the diseases of poverty and misery."

"Isn't anyone doing anything about it?" Melisande asked, studying the suddenly tense lines of his face.

"The government is struggling. A lot of private or international organizations are trying. But it's hard to make much headway when you have a population that is growing as fast as ours is, especially among the poor."

Alex glanced down briefly into Melisande's upturned face, and she sensed that a little of the tension within him eased.

"We are trying, in my company. A few years ago I started some programs to provide better housing and health care for our workers—day care for children, with decent, hot meals every day, so their mothers could earn some money for the family without worrying about them. We support some schools and offer scholarships to students who are able to overcome the incredible handicaps they face and qualify for college. But it's not enough. It helps, but it's not enough."

Alex shifted away from her to sit on the cement and stone wall that surrounded the area beneath the statue of Christ. There was something in his face that Melisande could only describe as sadness as he gazed out over the city he loved.

She went to sit beside him, drawn to him in a way that was different from anything she'd felt in his presence before. She was moved by the sympathy and compassion that could lead him, a hardheaded businessman, to invest company profits in programs that benefited the workers rather than lining the pockets of the stockholders. There were emotional depths to this man that she hadn't suspected.

"What's important is that people do *something*," she said softly. "No one can solve the world's problems all by himself. And, while we should never forget that there is suffering in the world, we also should never forget that there is great beauty, too, sometimes in the middle of the greatest suffering."

Again Alex turned to look at her, and this time there was something in the dark brown eyes Melisande couldn't interpret, something that reached out to her, asking a question she didn't understand. Then the hard line of his lips lifted in a gentle, quizzical smile.

"And what would a professor of history know about such things?" he asked.

Though the words sounded mocking, Melisande could detect no mockery in his voice. She stared out over the city while she searched for the words to explain herself.

"I think a history professor must know as much about human suffering as anyone," she said at last, picking her words carefully. "Not firsthand, not the way a social worker knows it. We know it as a part of human history. Terrible misery, disease, poverty—it's all there for the historian to see, no matter what era one is dealing with."

She turned back to face him. "You see, modern historians aren't concerned just with the generals and the politicians. A lot of work is being done to learn about the lives of the ordinary people who used to be forgotten in the history texts."

"Is that why you wrote about the Irish peasants and the potato famine?"

Alex hadn't taken his gaze from her face. There was something unsettling in that unwavering stare, something disturbing and demanding.

She shrugged, trying to fight off the impression. "I happened to pick up a book about the blight that hit the potato crop, which was the main source of food for the Irish poor. When I began to read about the heroism and self-sacrifice of many of the hardest-hit victims of that famine, I knew that I had to try to tell their story. Because in spite of it all, there was still love and caring and hope."

"Do you really believe love matters that much?"

The scornful note in Alex's voice seemed, to Melisande, to hide some other, more painful emotion.

"It mattered to many of the Irish peasants," she said softly. "It mattered to a lot of the people who came here, too. Love and hope were sometimes all that kept people going. Those two things are what make life worthwhile, no matter whether you're rich or poor."

Again she reached out to touch his arm. He glanced down at her hand then back at her. He seemed sad, as though her words had stirred some painful memory.

Rather than intrude on his thoughts, Melisande stared at the glittering city sprawling between lush forest and dazzling ocean.

"It really is incredibly beautiful," she said at last, when she couldn't bear to be silent any longer.

"You're right, it is incredibly beautiful." His voice was soft and warm, all trace of sadness banished as if it had never been.

Melisande turned back to him, smiling. He rose to his feet, pulling her up beside him.

"And you are beautiful," he said, "if slightly wind-blown. But I'm getting hungry. How about lunch?"

"Your compliments, gallant sir, do wonders for a girl's ego. Lunch sounds great." She laughed, and this time he laughed with her.

As they walked down the steps to the restaurant located on a lower level, Alex unself-consciously put his arm around her shoulder, drawing her against him as they walked. His gesture seemed one of friendly affection, and Melisande found herself relaxing comfortably against him, aware of his body as it moved beside hers, content in the comforting intimacy he offered, afraid even to think of the possiblity that there might be more.

They ordered fish and *caipirinhas*, the refreshing, dangerously tasty and beguiling drink made with limes, sugar, ice, and *cachaça*, the Brazilian liquor made with sugar cane.

In the breezy, sunny comfort of the outdoor restaurant, their conversation turned to Brazil's colorful history. Alex recounted some of his beloved country's story, from its time as a colony of Portugal, to its grandeur when the Portuguese king, ousted by Napoleon, moved the center of his empire to Rio, to Brazil's exciting growth as a nation with rubber plantations, the early gold and diamond mines, and the vast cattle ranches of the south.

Melisande watched Alex's face as he spoke, drawn by the enthusiasm that animated his features and brightened his dark eyes.

"You seem to know a lot about this country," she said when he paused.

"I love Brazil," he said softly, looking around him slowly as though savoring each part of the view. He turned back to her.

"My great-great-grandfather came here from France when he was just a poor young boy hoping to make his fortune. He worked hard, prospecting for gold and diamonds in what is now the state of Minas Gerais. He was lucky. He found what he was looking for, and had the ability to hang on to it. Unlike some of the old families, we've been able to hang on to what he built."

"And what do you do now?" Melisande asked. His enthusiasm intrigued her. "You mentioned something about your company."

There was no mistaking the surprise in Alex's glance. "What do you mean, what do I do?"

"I mean, what sort of work do you do? You told me you were a businessman the first day we met, and now you've mentioned your company."

"You don't know?" Alex's surprise was now combined with quite obvious disbelief.

"No, I don't. Am I supposed to?"

His disbelief irritated her. Why was she supposed to know what he did? And why didn't he believe her?

"I'm the president of Robeson and Company," he said, as though that explained everything.

In spite of her irritation, Melisande burst out laughing.

"I think," she said, "we're having a problem communicating. What does Robeson and Company do?"

"You mean you *really* don't know?"

Melisande shook her head. She was beginning to suspect she'd just wounded Alex's pride, which would account for the disbelief in his voice.

"Robeson and Company," he said, as though he were explaining a difficult proposition to a backward child, "is one of Brazil's major jewelers. We still have our own gold and diamond mines, as well as mines for some of the other gemstones found here. We also have shops in most of the large cities of the world, and we're a major exporter of fine jewelry and gemstones."

Melisande hoped her smile was properly conciliatory. "Well, how do you expect someone living on a university professor's salary to know anything about Robeson and Company? I must say, it sounds rather fascinating."

Her smile worked. Alex seemed to relax, though a hint of his distrust lingered in the shadows in his dark eyes.

"It is," he said. "Would you like to see our main shop and the workrooms some day?"

She didn't have to waste time considering the invitation—she accepted instantly. "Yes, thank you. I'd like that."

It would be interesting to visit a world-class jewelry store. She'd never done more than peer in the window at Tiffany's in New York, and she certainly had never had the money to buy fine jewelry.

"Tomorrow?"

"No, I can't." Melisande shook her head regretfully. "I have an appointment to visit a professor of Brazilian history tomorrow. How about the day after?" she added hastily. She didn't want to demean his invitation. And she did want to visit his shop.

Alex nodded in agreement. "Would ten o'clock be all right?"

"That would be fine." Melisande pushed her chair back. "Now, how about a stroll along some of the paths here?" she said.

Since the waiter had already brought the check, Alex simply left some bills on the table, then rose and came to hold her chair for her.

Melisande stood. When she turned to thank him, she found that he'd stepped closer to her and was staring down at her, a thoughtful, puzzled look in his eyes.

For an instant their eyes held, then Melisande dropped her gaze. The intensity she'd seen in Alex's, combined with his proximity to her, were too disturbing to face for long. Nervously, she wet her lips with her tongue and instantly regretted it. It aroused memories that made her cheeks flush, her heart rate speed up considerably.

She was relieved and, to her chagrin, disappointed when he stepped back.

"What about that stroll?" he asked lightly.

In the train going down the mountain Melisande found that the sun, the lunch, and the stroll had induced a pleasant drowsiness and a totally unfamiliar feeling of peace. She glanced up, only to find Alex staring at her with a soft smile on his lips and a question in his eyes.

There seemed no need for words between them. Melisande smiled gently, content in the comfortable silence. Alex's eyes softened, and his smile lifted slightly; then he casually sat back against the seat.

Stretching his long legs out before him and his arm along the seat back, he turned his head to gaze out the window on the other side of the car.

Melisande studied the sharp lines of his profile, the heavy mass of dark hair, tossed now by the wind, that fell across his brow. He seemed, for the first time since she'd known him, totally relaxed and at peace.

She started to reach out, wanting to touch him, to feel the strength of those lean muscles, the warmth of that sun-bronzed skin. At the last second she drew back, clutching her hand against her chest as though she'd burned it by reaching too near a flame.

Suddenly, she understood why she felt so at peace with him—she was starting to fall in love with a man she was only just beginning to know.

FIVE

The entrance of Robeson and Company was an impressively modern creation of glass, chrome, marble, and dark, plush carpets.

The receptionist smiled brightly when Melisande presented herself. "Oh, yes, Dr. Merrick, Senhor Robeson said you were to be shown up immediately when you arrived."

The sophisticated young secretary who eventually showed Melisande into Alex's office explained that Senhor Robeson would be back in a minute and apologized for the delay. She offered Melisande a cup of coffee.

As Melisande sipped the coffee, she studied the office. As sleekly modern and luxurious as the lobby, it almost reeked of power and wealth and influence. It wasn't the sort of place where she fitted in, but it suited Alex perfectly.

Setting her coffee aside, she rose and went to the window that stretched across the far wall. The view was spectacular.

She was bent over a display case, admiring a heavy gold collar set with emeralds, when Alex returned. She glanced up, then caught her breath at the sharp physical reaction that coursed through her at the sight of him. He came toward her, moving easily, a man totally at home in this elegant setting. His light gray, perfectly tailored suit disguised but could not hide his powerful build, and the lean lines of his face further emphasized the overall impression of masculine strength.

"I'm sorry to have kept you waiting, but I see my secretary has taken care of you in my absence."

He was at her side, smiling down at her with a casual friendliness that carried a hint of something more tantalizing. The smile, the warmth in his eyes, and his nearness were a disturbing combination. Melisande had to fight to maintain her composure.

"I've been admiring your display." Melisande was pleased that her voice carried no hint of how easily she was affected by his presence. "I've never seen anything quite like it."

He nodded at the necklace in the display case "That collar won our company a prize in an international competition among jewelers. We made it for a woman who requested something especially for her, then refused to accept it because she considered it too simple."

His lips quirked in the brief smile Melisande was beginning to recognize. "When it won the prize she decided she wanted it, after all. She was furious when I refused to sell it to her."

"I can't imagine anyone not wanting it," said Melisande truthfully, studying the heavy, shining gold collar set with randomly placed, deep green emeralds. "But not everyone could wear something like that. I think I prefer this simpler necklace over here."

Alex followed her to a case containing, among other items, a stunning necklace displayed on a bed of dark blue velvet. A fine band of white gold dropped in a gentle curve to cradle an oval blue stone whose facets caught the light with a dazzling brilliance that matched the fiery sparkle of the diamonds set beside it.

"That's an aquamarine, isn't it?" Melisande asked, pointing. "It's so delicate, and yet it seems almost alive with light."

Alex leaned closer. His arm brushed hers; then he stepped away, seemingly unaware that even that slight touch had been enough to send heat shooting through her. Melisande kept her gaze fixed on the necklace, hoping he wouldn't see the flush his touch had brought to her cheeks.

"You have excellent taste." His voice was as soft and intimate as a caress. "I'm rather proud of that necklace. I think it's one of my better designs."

Melisande glanced up to find him studying her rather than the necklace.

"You look surprised," he said.

"I guess I just never pictured you designing jewelry," she admitted. "Even when you said you ran a jewelry business."

He grinned and Melisande's stomach muscles tightened involuntarily. She looked away, disconcerted. How could any man affect her so much with so little effort? To hide her reaction, she moved to another display case.

"Is there much demand for special pieces?" she asked. "This necklace, for instance, is different from anything else I've seen. Does it have a history?"

The necklace she pointed to was formed of a series of gold leaves, each connected to the next so that they formed a flexible chain just long enough to lie like a collar around the throat of a beautiful woman. Between the leaves in front, jewels in a variety of colors dangled: purple, blue, deep red, green, pink, and amber. Diamonds topped each gem where it was connected to the gold chain. The whole made a stunningly ornate piece that glowed and sparkled on its bed of wine-colored velvet.

"It was one of my father's creations."

Alex came to stand beside her. He scarcely glanced in the display case, but continued to study her, his eyes dark and unreadable, a slight, disconcerting smile on his lips. "It was designed to display some of Brazil's riches. The leaves are the shape of coffee leaves, and coffee is one of the country's major exports. The gems are all from our mines here— diamonds, amethysts, aquamarines, garnets, topazes, and tourmalines. Do you like it?"

"Well . . ." Melisande hesitated. "Um . . . Not really. It's a little ornate for my taste, but I'm sure it would be stunning on the right woman."

His sudden burst of laughter startled her. She glanced up to find his face alight, his eyes sparkling.

"You're certainly honest, aren't you? Even knowing that my father designed it, you're willing to admit you don't like it. Don't let my mother ever hear you say that. She adores the thing."

"And you don't?"

Again he smiled at her. "No. I happen to agree with you. It's too ornate, but it *is* stunning, and it's an unusual way to show off some of Brazil's gemstones. But come, let me show you our workrooms."

Taking her arm gently, he led her to a door at the far side of the room. Melisande could feel the warmth of his fingers against her skin. She didn't realize she'd been holding her breath until he released her to let her lead the way down a narrow, circular staircase that led to a lower floor.

As she started down Melisande forced herself to concentrate on placing each foot on the narrow steps. It wasn't easy when she was so intensely aware of the tall man behind her. At the bottom Alex moved past her to unlock the door in front of them.

"These are the workrooms where we make the jewelry we sell. Usually our visitors are led through a hall on the other side, where they can look through windows into one of the shops that does the simpler pieces. But I'll introduce you to some of our craftsmen who do the most complex and valuable pieces."

The first workroom was a small, well-lighted area dominated by a long wooden table against one wall. Two older men sat hunched over the work in front of them. They glanced up, then smiled in respectful recognition of their employer. Alex exchanged a few words of Portuguese with them, before drawing Melisande to the side of the older man.

"Fernando is working on a special order from a woman in Rome. It has taken us quite a while to assemble the necessary stones, but now it should be done in a few weeks."

Melisande studied the pieces of gold, each with gaping holes, lying on the worn and battered wood. "Why did it take so long to get the stones?"

"It's not always easy to get high-quality diamonds and aquamarines of the shape, size, and color we need. In a necklace of this quality all the stones must be equally fine, or the value of the piece declines sharply. One poorer quality stone, which might be beautiful in another necklace, can reduce the price by thousands of dollars. Here, take a look at these stones and you'll see what I mean."

He bent and unrolled a bundle of velvet on the table. Melisande gasped at the sudden blaze of sparkling light which leaped from the blue and white gemstones. Tentatively she reached out to pick up the large aquamarine that lay in the center of the collection.

"I didn't know a piece of stone could be so beautiful, so full of light."

Her voice was scarcely louder than a whisper. The dark blue stone in her hand blazed as each precisely cut facet reflected the light.

She glanced up to find Alex studying her, as though seeking an answer to a question he hadn't asked. His gaze was more puzzling than disturbing, but she could detect no hint of the thought behind it.

Melisande returned the aquamarine to its place. Striving for a note of casual curiosity, she said, "What would something like this cost?"

"This?" Alex's eyes darkened. Suddenly, they seemed almost as hard and glitteringly bright as the gems on the velvet. "This particular necklace will cost around five hundred thousand dollars."

He laughed at Melisande's startled gasp.

"A half a million dollars? For one necklace?" Was it her imagination, or had there been a sharp, hard edge to his laughter?

"And at that, not anywhere near the most expensive thing we've ever done. But of course most of what we sell runs for a few hundred or a few thousand dollars, no more."

Melisande shook her head in stunned disbelief.

"Even a necklace worth a few hundred dollars would be a major purchase for me. I can't imagine having enough money to think of buying anything more valuable than that."

"Really? Most people can imagine it just fine."

This time Melisande was sure. There really *was* a sharp edge to his voice.

"Come," Alex said, turning to the door, "let me show you our salesroom."

The room was an open area that seemed to stretch on forever, divided only by tall, well-lighted glass display cabinets. Between the cabinets, chairs had been grouped around small tables, providing semiprivate areas for customers while they considered their purchases. A number of the tables were taken by small groups of people bent over large, velvet-covered trays of jewels. Melisande could see several women holding hand mirrors while they studied the effect of a necklace or earrings.

Alex had no sooner seated her at a table than two attendants, obviously acting on prior orders, brought several of the velvet-covered jewel trays. Melisande had to stifle a gasp of surprise at the bewildering array of jewelry and gems displayed in neatly ordered boxes on the trays.

Together they studied the contents of the trays, and Alex explained special settings or different cuts of the gemstones. There were simple pairs of stud earrings, ornate bracelets, elegant cuff links, glittering pieces that would be appropriate only on the most formal occasion and others that could be used for everyday wear. Alex had even included a few pieces that weren't jewelry—cigarette cases, letter openers, costly paperweights.

"It's rather intimidating," she admitted, ruefully meeting Alex's dark eyes across the table. "And yet, I can see why people would be tempted by all this. I had no idea there could be so much beauty and variety. It makes me start lusting for diamonds and emeralds myself."

She said it as a joke, but Alex didn't laugh. Instead, he looked down at the velvet trays, as if unwilling to meet her gaze.

"It's a world apart," he said at last, slowly, as if choosing his words carefully, "but it's as old as civilization, maybe older. Man has been making ornaments for himself for thousands of years, first from bone and feathers, then from gold, silver, and beautiful stones."

He lifted a glittering earring with a diamond and pearl pendant and studied it, his dark eyebrows drawn together in a frown.

"I believe we respond to these jewels because they touch that part within us that knows what is beautiful. Our greed, when we suddenly realize the value they carry, comes after."

His features tensed suddenly. The line of his mouth thinned and grew hard as the stones he held. Abruptly, he tossed the earring back with its mate and said, "But the greed comes. It always comes."

Before Melisande could respond he raised his head abruptly and signaled to one of the assistants. While he gave an order in Portuguese, she studied the strong lines of his face, now drawn into a cool, expressionless mask. There was no sign of the relaxed, understanding smile she'd seen on his lips earlier.

When he turned back to her, Melisande said gently, "Not everyone is motivated by greed. Perhaps you see more of it than most of us do, but it isn't what drives the majority of people, you know."

He arched one eyebrow cynically, but said only, "Perhaps you're right."

At that moment the assistant returned with a small box. She handed it to Alex before withdrawing with a friendly smile at Melisande.

Without opening the box Alex handed it to Melisande.

"I thought you might be interested in these," he said.

Curious, Melisande took the box after one puzzled glance at his expressionless face. The box was a standard, velvet-covered jeweler's box with a hinged lid. Inside a pair of earrings lay on its velvet bed.

"They're lovely," said Melisande softly as she took one earring out of the box and held it to the light.

A small triangle composed of three small, brilliant diamonds was backed by a screw post of yellow gold. The pendant, a tourmaline of a rich, blue-green color, was cut in a long, narrow rectangle. Held up to the light, the flashing diamonds made a striking contrast with the lush color of the delicate tourmaline. They weren't flashy earrings, but they were elegant and would attract attention in any gathering.

"I rather thought you would like them," said Alex.

He watched her for a moment. The expressionless mask was gone from his face, but Melisande could not interpret the look she caught from his dark eyes as they met hers.

He leaned across the little table and gently took the earring from her unresisting fingers, then held it so it sparkled in the light. He glanced at the glittering piece of jewelry for a moment before his gaze moved to hold hers.

Puzzled, and suddenly tense, Melisande was totally unprepared when he stretched out his hand to hold the earring against her earlobe. His fingers grazed the line of her jaw, then rested softly against her neck. His touch, intimate and gentle, burned against her delicate skin.

"I was right. The color of the tourmalines matches your beautiful eyes." His voice matched his touch, intimate and gentle, and Melisande could feel the warmth beginning to rise in her cheeks. "But you should wear your lovely hair down, instead of up in that formal bun."

Irritated at her unbidden reaction, Melisande turned her head away and, without meeting his eyes, reached to take the earring from him. Her fingers trembled briefly as they met his, but he offered no resistance as he relinquished the earring.

"It's a good thing I don't have much use for such lovely jewelry," she said lightly. "Otherwise I might be tempted by them."

She kept her eyes down as she returned the earring to its place and closed the box.

"And you're not tempted? What a shame. They are a gift to you. I picked them out myself, and I would be saddened to think you might never wear them."

Melisande's head jerked up. She felt the flush receeding from her cheeks, leaving her cold. There was a cold, mocking note in Alex's voice that rang strangely.

"I don't accept gifts like that, Alex," she said.

"Why won't you accept the earrings? They're just trinkets, and they suit you."

"Expensive trinkets. And frankly rather insulting after your comment about greed."

It was Alex's look of disbelief that brought a surge of anger rushing to her defense. What kind of woman did he think she was? Some gold digger interested only in the jewelry she could get out of him? She'd only learned about his work two days before. The offer of such an expensive gift was more brutally painful than a slap in the face.

Melisande carefully laid the box with the earrings on one of the trays before her, then rose with graceful dignity. She was careful to keep her anger from her face; she had no wish to show any of the other people in the room that she was upset.

Alex scrambled quickly to his feet, but before he could speak she said, "I'll find my own way out. Whatever your intention with the gift, I want to thank you for your time and the tour. I doubt I would ever have visited a jewelry store on my own. And thank you again for the lunch on the Corcovado."

The memory of that bit at her, sharp and hurtful.

"I . . . ," she started to say more, then stopped. She'd been about to say she was sorry, because she'd hoped they might, eventually, be something more than friends.

"If you were going to offer me a gift," she said, "I would have preferred daisies."

With that, she turned and walked away, achingly aware that he remained standing by the table, watching her. Her anger and pride carried her across a display room that suddenly seemed enormous and down to the lobby, but once she was settled in a taxi she only had strength enough to give the driver her address before she collapsed into tears.

SIX

For three days Melisande threw herself into her work with an intensity designed to force all other thoughts from her mind. She took her usual morning run, then spent long hours hunched over old records in the archive where Marta worked, arriving when the archive opened and going home only when it closed.

Once Marta was moved to protest such grueling work. "You can't spend twelve hours a day here!" she objected, a worried frown on her face.

"I have a lot of work to do," was all Melisande said before turning back to her books.

After a light dinner that Senhora Amado would have ready, Melisande closed herself up in the apartment's study and continued working.

It was true she had a great deal to do and little time in which to do it, but Melisande knew her dedication wasn't all because of her concern for her work.

It certainly wasn't achieving what she had hoped— she wasn't forgetting Alex Robeson.

Even while she ran along the beach or struggled with the Portuguese in an old book, thoughts of him forced themselves into her consciousness. And as she lay in bed at night an image of his face would pass before her mind's eye. Sometimes he seemed to be laughing, sometimes watching her with distrust.

Whatever his expression, the image tormented her.

What was most disturbing was her realization that she cared a very great deal about what he thought of her. It wasn't just that she was hurt by his assumption that she would accept a costly gift. She was hurt even more by the knowledge that she had never mattered as much to him as he had mattered to her.

To be sure, he had offered her a gift that would be considered enormously generous in her world, if not in his. But he had done so with the air of a man who had given similar gifts on numerous occasions, and always with the same result.

He'd been sure she would accept the earrings. The expression on his face had said clearly that, whatever else lay between them, she would not be able to resist a gift of such valuable jewelry.

She was too honest with herself not to admit she was attracted to Alex. After the visit to the Corcovado, she'd even thought for a moment that she could fall in love with him. Certainly she had been surprised and moved by his willingness to talk openly with her about things she suspected he discussed with few people.

And it wasn't just the physical attraction between them that drew her. He was an intelligent, complex, and passionate man, totally different from anyone she had ever known. But he had insulted her with his "gift," wounded her deeply with his doubt; and it was going to take a while for her to recover from it.

Regret was a useless emotion, but it plagued Melisande anyway. Since work was the only antidote she knew, she dug into her books in the hope that she could somehow lose the hurt among all the written records of lives and loves so long past that the only pain remaining in them was trapped in fading ink on yellowed, crumbling pages few would ever see.

It wasn't much help, but it was the only escape she knew.

On the third evening after the disastrous visit to Alex Robeson's company, Melisande was sitting in the study unable to work and musing unhappily on thoughts she knew she'd be better off ignoring entirely when she was jerked back to reality by a knock on the door. Before she had a chance to speak, the door swung open and a hand, clutching a bunch of daisies, was extended into the doorway.

The hand was followed, after a moment, by its owner, one Alex Robeson, looking shamefaced— and incredibly handsome.

"I thought I'd give you a chance to shoot my hand off before I risked my head," he said, smiling enchantingly. "And the daisies only cost me a few cents from a street vendor, so you can't possibly complain of my extravagance."

In spite of herself Melisande found her lips lifting in a sudden, happy smile. "They still don't guarantee your safety, you know."

"I was afraid that would be the case." Alex's forehead wrinkled in rueful regret. "I have a white handkerchief in my pocket. Should I wave that instead?"

Why, thought Melisande, should I feel so ridiculously happy to see him? I have no reason to trust him, every reason to try and forget him.

Out loud she said, "It's not necessary at the moment, but I would be careful if I were you. If you've come to apologize I might consider putting the shotgun to the side. But I warn you—I'll keep it handy, just in case."

"Fair enough." His face relaxed into a friendly smile. "And I *did* come to apologize. I was completely out of line and I'm sorry."

He moved to sit in a chair a safe distance from her on the other side of the table.

Head cocked to one side, Melisande studied him thoughtfully.

"Perhaps," she said slowly, "you didn't really mean the gift to be so, so . . ."

"Insulting," he offered.

"Insulting." Melisande nodded, watching him. There was no hint of mockery on his face. "But the offer of an expensive gift, coming right after your comments on greed, *was* an insult. It hurt."

Alex's lips twisted in a penitent grimace. "The gift was in bad taste, I admit, but I hadn't intended it to be insulting. I can't tell you how much I regret hurting your feelings."

His face brightened, and he smiled hesitantly. "Since I can't tell you, I thought you might let me show you, instead."

"Show me?"

"Will you let me take you to dinner? Please?"

Melisande chewed her lip doubtfully.

"I promise to be on my best behavior."

She couldn't help laughing at his meek promise. He really did seem to regret having hurt her feelings, and she was more than ready to forgive him, if only because these last few days had been such a misery.

"I already told Senhora Amado to stop making your dinner," he added.

"You what?"

"I wasn't sure you'd accept my invitation, but I thought the threat of going hungry if you didn't would help convince you to be . . . kind."

"That's outrageous!"

"You're right," he agreed meekly, "it is."

"I don't think I want to go, thank you," said Melisande, head held high. She was fighting against an almost dizzying sense of relief . . . and she had every intention of going to dinner with Alex.

"I already made reservations for the best table in the rooftop restaurant of the Meridien," he pleaded.

"The Meridien? That enormous hotel at the end of Copacabana beach?"

"The view is the best of any restaurant's in town."

"Well . . ."

"Good," said Alex with satisfaction. "I have my driver downstairs waiting for us. Take all the time you need to change."

She didn't need long. Happiness seemed to have lent her wings. Her hair was already neatly tied up in her usual bun. Once again her glasses were replaced with contact lenses. The slacks and T-shirt she wore were quickly exchanged for a silk sheath dress in white and pink. White, high-heeled sandals on her feet and a touch of eyeshadow and she was ready to go.

Instead of the Mercedes, a black limousine with driver was waiting for them outside the building. As Melisande settled back against the soft leather seat, she gave a sigh of contentment.

All the misery of the past three days might never have been. She wasn't sure just what Alex's apology and dinner invitation meant for their future relationship, but at least he cared enough to have made the effort.

As he settled in beside her, Melisande glanced at him, and as quickly looked away. Despite the emotional injury he'd caused her, nothing had changed—he still had the ability to affect her just by being near her.

The driver closed the doors, shutting out the heat and humidity of a typical Rio summer night and enclosing them in a cool, dark, intimate cocoon of luxury.

To Melisande, the drive from Ipanema across to Copacabana and then along the broad avenue that followed the sweep of Copacabana beach seemed to pass in an instant. They didn't speak much, but she was content just to be with him and to watch the passing scene. Sitting this close to Alex, she wasn't sure she would have been able to carry on any intelligent conversation, anyway.

Dinner passed in a similar haze. Melisande knew they talked about a dozen things over their leisurely meal and through the coffee and liqueurs. But all she could remember afterward was the thousands of lights she could see through the broad windows of the rooftop restaurant, as well as a sense of happiness that was so intense it almost hurt. She couldn't even remember how she got home, though they must have returned in Alex's limousine.

What she did remember, however, was Alex taking her in his arms in front of her apartment door. She came to him willingly, as though it were what she had waited for throughout the evening. His arms felt so right about her—strong, yet gentle and secure.

Melisande found her arms fit as easily around him as his did around her. There was no false movement, no hesitant fumbling. When their lips met it was as though they were drawn together by an irresistible force as natural as magnetism.

And just as elemental as magnetism was the fire their embrace ignited. To Melisande—already intensely aware of him, of the way he moved and spoke, of the heat and subtle, masculine smell of him—the sudden, demanding heat that rose in her, curling from the center of her being to reach every inch of her responsive body, was no more than the natural, unavoidable response to his kisses.

His mouth crushed hers, forcing her to open to his probing demands. And when she surrendered, he took without remorse. Melisande met him eagerly. When his lips moved from hers briefly, as though he were pausing to catch his breath, she whimpered in protest, then began her own exploration.

She trailed kisses along his jaw and down his throat until blocked by the collar of his shirt. Though he had obviously shaved again that evening, the coarse, dark beard that was just beginning to reappear rasped tantalizingly against her lips. She ran her fingers through her hair and rose on tiptoe, leaning into him, trusting him to hold her, wanting to feel the hard, masculine length of him against her.

At last they drew apart, reluctantly. Through her own physical turmoil Melisande could feel him trembling as though fighting for control of his body. She stretched up to brush another kiss, less fierce but no less arousing, across his lips. His breath, rushed and uneven, was warm against her swollen mouth.

"Good night, Melisande," he said. "I'm glad you liked the daisies."

He released her and started to step away. Melisande, dazed, cried out an inarticulate protest and reached out to hold him. As though snatching forbidden fruit, Alex bent to brush another swift kiss across her lips, then firmly pushed her away.

In a moment he was gone, leaving her to try to regain her self-control alone.

Sleep came late that night, and her dreams gave her little rest.

The next morning Melisande found herself unable to concentrate on the work before her. Anxious to find an excuse to distract her thoughts from the distinctly provocative trend they insisted on taking, she called Maria Sebastian, the dress designer she had met at Marta Araujo's party.

Maria crowed with pleasure at Melisande's announced intention of buying a dress.

"I'll find something special for you," she promised. "And you must let me take you to lunch afterward.

"I insist," she added imperatively when Melisande tried to protest. "I already asked Marta for your telephone number because I wanted to see more of you. Now you have given me the chance."

The shop proved easy to find, one of a series of small, elegant, and, Melisande had no doubt, expensive shops on one of the side streets of Ipanema. She was struck by its air of modern elegance and exclusivity. Only a few dresses were hung on the racks, brightly colored cocktail and evening gowns whose shimmering fabrics were reflected again and again in the mirrors that covered the walls.

Melisande had to ring for someone to open the shop door, and though she could see no one within, the door buzzed open and she stepped into the cool interior.

Before she could say anything, Maria Sebastian burst from the back exclaiming, "Melisande! I'm so glad you came!"

She took Melisande by the arm and led her toward the back room, almost bouncing in her enthusiasm.

"I've had such fun this morning, picking out some dresses for you to try on," she said as they settled into one of the dressing rooms. "Please don't feel compelled to buy anything. I shall feel very bad if you do. But I love it when my friends are as pretty as you. They make my clothes even more beautiful. And you have excellent taste—I saw that the other night. You will be dangerous to our Brazilian men. That will be good for them."

It was impossible not to share Maria's happy

laughter. Melisande quickly found that Maria had not wasted time that morning; there were a variety of dresses for her to try, ranging from simple sundresses to stunningly sophisticated gowns for evening wear.

As one lovely creation succeeded another, Melisande became more and more confused. She had always liked clothes and had taken great care in selecting her wardrobe, choosing pieces that were of good quality and that would blend with what she already owned. But this time every dress she tried on made her want to buy it.

"It's impossible!" she finally exclaimed, throwing up her hands in mock despair. "You're only confusing me with all these choices. I want almost everything I've tried on, and I don't even have any place to wear most of them!"

"I *knew* they would look good on you. Didn't I say so?" Maria looked smugly pleased with herself. "But I have saved my favorite for last. The others are all very nice, but this will be the best."

She waved an elegant hand, then gave swift commands in Portuguese to an assistant who was gathering up some of the discarded gowns.

"Though I do think," she continued, "that you ought to consider taking the red dress for daytime. It's very becoming, and I selected the fabric so that it would travel well."

"In another century, Maria, you would have been burned at the stake for a witch," said Melisande, grinning at her new friend. "Of all of them, I had just about decided that I wouldn't be able to live without the red dress."

The only reply she got was a conspiratorial twinkle from brilliant green eyes before the assistant came back. She stopped a short distance before Melisande, gracefully held out the dress she carried, then carefully pulled out the shimmering folds of a full skirt.

Melisande could only gasp as the dress's fabric caught the light and turned from a rich green to a dazzling, hypnotic flow of color that changed from green to blue-green to blue to silver as the delicate fabric shifted beneath the designer's hands.

"Did I not tell you? It is the best of them all, and it will suit you very well. Only someone as slender as you could wear a dress cut like this, and the fabric will be stunning with your dark hair."

The dress was everything Maria promised. Melisande, gazing at herself in the mirror, scarcely recognized the woman she saw, so different was she from the cool, elegant woman she was accustomed to seeing.

The woman who gazed back at her was still cool and elegant, but there was a new and previously unknown provocative sensuousness, a hint of something—dangerous—that she had never seen in herself before. Perhaps it was the way the dress left one shoulder bare, or the way it clung to, then stirred around her slim body, that made the difference. But the difference was unmistakably there.

Bemused, she continued to stare at herself, speechless. She imagined wearing the dress to a party. She was standing in a crowd of faceless, chattering bodies while a man walked toward her, drawn to her through the surrounding crush of people. She could feel his dark eyes on her, feel his aura of overwhelming masculinity, see his face—

Abruptly she came to her senses, self-consciously aware of the uncomfortable flush that was spreading up her throat and across her cheeks. She had come dress-shopping in an attempt to get Alex Robeson out of her thoughts. She didn't want to think of him now, and certainly not in relation to the provocative dress she was wearing!

Maria suddenly moved from the corner in which she had been sitting and came to stand beside Melisande.

"Did I not say it was the best? The dress was made for you. Other women have tried it, but it has never suited anyone as it suits you. And it fits perfectly." The redhead's voice was alive with her delight in her creation. A moment later she added, laughing, "Melisande, you're blushing!"

Melisande blushed an even darker rose at the friendly amusement in the other woman's tinkling laugh.

"You should not blush. You are only seeing a you that has been hidden. You will break dozens of hearts, and it will be great fun to see you do it."

Melisande turned away, confused by what she had seen in the mirror and the thoughts that image had conjured up.

"It's beautiful, Maria, the most beautiful thing I have ever worn. But it's not me," she said quickly, trying to check the designer's enthusiasm. "I wouldn't feel comfortable wearing a dress like this. I'm a historian. I don't wear such things. I don't mean to be rude, but it just isn't me."

For a moment Melisande thought her new friend would be angry at the rejection of the dress, but the volatile redhead simply smiled in sympathetic comprehension. If she didn't know all that had gone through Melisande's thoughts, she could probably guess at some of it and was intelligent enough not to take offense.

"I am sorry, of course. But you must decide. Perhaps you should think about it. I will put the dress aside in case you change your mind. After seeing it on you, I couldn't bear to sell it to just anyone, anyway."

She turned aside to give swift instructions to the assistant, who had remained quietly in the corner, allowing Melisande time to recover her composure while she carefully removed the dress.

The red dress was quickly boxed and paid for. At Maria's suggestion, Melisande made arrangements to have it delivered to her apartment later that day, then dutifully followed Maria out the door for a well-deserved lunch.

SEVEN

Lunch was at a small French restaurant near Maria's shop. It didn't take long for them to get into a lively discussion that started with high fashion and ranged through topics concerning clothing until it eventually arrived at the subject of jewelry.

"You must buy at least one beautiful piece of jewelry while you are here," Maria insisted, "even if it means you eat soup for a month!"

Melisande laughed. Maria was always so emphatic about everything.

"Alex took me through his store," she said without thinking. "I found it all rather overwhelming. I don't think I would ever be able to choose, even if I had the money to buy something special, because everything was so beautiful."

"Alex took you through his store?" Maria's eyes widened in obvious surprise.

"Yes, and it was quite an experience. But I've never visited any of the other jewelry stores, so I don't have anything to compare it to. Are there any good small stores that you would recommend?" she added, trying to change the subject.

"When did Alex invite you to visit his store?" Maria was not going to be sidetracked.

"Uh, when he took me up the Corcovado." Melisande could have bitten her tongue, but the words were already out.

"He took you up the Corcovado, too?" Maria was alight with interest, like a hunting dog on a strong scent.

"He wanted to show me the view of the city," said Melisande lamely. "Have you known him a long time?" she asked, trying to change the direction, if not the topic, of their discussion.

"Since we were kids," said Maria frankly. "But I've never known him to take anyone up the Corcovado, and he would *never* take a woman as pretty as you through his shop."

"Really?" said Melisande, startled. "Why is that?"

"It's too dangerous. Alex has had bad luck with the women he's fallen in love with. Once they find out he's the wealthy owner of one of the world's leading jewelry companies, they invariably start wanting him to give them something. Or lots of somethings. Sometimes they even find out who he is before they meet him, then go out of their way to get an introduction."

Maria shook her head in disgust.

Despite herself, Melisande found herself wanting to hear more about Alex.

"Poor Alex," Maria continued sadly. "I sometimes think he would have been happier if he'd inherited just about any other kind of business in the world. Of course, he's a brilliant designer, but still . . ."

She eyed Melisande uncertainly, as though trying to decide what she should say next.

"Alex has become rather cynical about women," she said at last. "At one time he even designed a special bracelet to give to all his ex-girlfriends. It was made of gold and set with an amethyst."

She laughed suddenly.

"I was at a party once where three women, all incredibly beautiful, showed up, each wearing one of those bracelets. They were all mad as hell, and everybody else was embarrassed. But Alex seemed to think it was a good joke."

"But that's terrible!" Melisande exclaimed. "Though I don't know whether to feel sorrier for Alex or for the women," she added.

"I know what you mean," said Maria. "But Alex isn't cruel. It's just that he's been hurt too many times by women who are dazzled by all those jewels. He's a good friend, and always has been, and I would like nothing better than to see him happily married to the right woman. It's what all his friends want for him, though I confess I'm beginning to wonder if we'll ever get our wish that he'll fall in love at last."

She tilted her head, studying Melisande thoughtfully, then shrugged like someone throwing off a load of doubts.

"Though I admit," she added darkly, "that I've never forgiven him for the tree frogs."

"Tree frogs?"

Maria grinned, but Melisande sensed that her new friend was eager to change the subject, as though she was embarrassed to have divulged so much personal information about Alex.

"One time when I was about eight he put about a dozen of these little, tiny tree frogs down the back of my dress." Maria laughed, then shuddered theatrically. "He'd been collecting them in the garden for days. I thought I'd go crazy before I got the last of them off me."

Melisande couldn't help laughing. She'd seen the bitter side of Alex when he had tried to give her the earrings. Though she had only known him a short time, it wasn't hard to imagine the brighter, more carefree side of him, the side that would have led a small boy to put tree frogs down little girls' dresses.

She knew which Alex attracted her. But how much did she really know about him?

"My brother used to be just about as bad," said Maria, discreetly changing the subject. "If you have a brother you know what I mean."

Melisande followed Maria's lead gratefully. She wanted to know more about this man she had met only days before and who attracted her so powerfully. But Maria was not the person to ask. At least, not yet.

Through sheer force of will Melisande was able to get a fair amount of work done that afternoon. Catalina had obtained for her a photocopy of a journal written by a woman who had come as an immigrant to Brazil in the mid eighteen hundreds. The journal was similar to many Melisande had seen written by American immigrant and pioneer women in the last century, but the simple story of sacrifice, hardship, and hope still had the power to move her.

She was engrossed in her reading when Alex suddenly appeared at her side and bent down to plant a kiss on the side of her neck, just below her ear.

"Alex!"

"A kiss to awaken a sleeping beauty, no more!"

"I wasn't sleeping, I was working. And you interrupted me!"

"This isn't work," he said, waving at the piles of papers, books, and documents before her. "This is slavery. And *I* am here to rescue you."

"Rescue me? How?" Melisande couldn't help laughing at the teasing light in Alex's dark eyes. *This*, she thought suddenly, *is how he must have looked when he put the tree frogs down Maria's dress.*

"Dinner, of course." Alex sat in the chair beside her with an airy assumption of dignity. "I introduced you to the Corcovado. I now propose to introduce you to *feijoada.*"

Melisande frowned. "I don't remember reading about it in the guide books."

"Not unless you read the restaurant section. It's a typical Brazilian dish and not to be missed."

"And I, I presume, am not going to miss it," said Melisande, amused.

"I know the best place in Rio for *feijoada.* It's a little hole in the wall where no self-respecting tourist would go, and which no self-respecting *Carioca* in the know would miss."

Before Melisande could reply, the housekeeper knocked on the door, then came in carrying two dress boxes, both prominently displaying Maria's logo. One box must contain the dress she had bought that morning, but Melisande couldn't imagine what the second box held.

"But I only bought one dress," she protested. "The messenger must have delivered the other box by mistake."

When Senhora Amado simply looked puzzled,

Melisande switched to her abysmal Portuguese, trying to explain that she was expecting one box, not two, and that the messenger shouldn't leave until she got it straightened out.

"Let me help," Alex volunteered. He rattled off a quick explanation in Portuguese.

To Melisande's surprise, the housekeeper shook her head firmly before replying.

"She says," said Alex, turning back to her, "that the messenger was very sure both boxes were for you. He said there's a note attached to one of them. And here it is," he added, plucking the envelope from its ribbon and handing it to Melisande.

As she opened the envelope, Melisande had a sinking feeling she knew what was in the extra box. She was right.

"Oh, dear," she said in distress. "Maria has sent me a second dress, one I tried on today but didn't buy."

Alex looked surprised, then hastened to defend his childhood friend. "She's not trying to force you to buy, you know. If she sent the dress she had a good reason."

"I know she's not trying to be pushy," Melisande admitted with a sigh. "She says that after seeing the dress on me this morning she can't bear to see it on anyone else so she's giving it to me as a gift. She says I'll be a good advertisement for her."

Melisande caught Alex's curious stare, then looked away, blushing. She could remember all too clearly how the dress had made her feel and the thoughts it had generated.

"I'm curious to see this dress," said Alex. "If

there is one thing Maria is always right about, it's clothes."

Before Melisande realized what he was doing, he had opened the box. She jumped up quickly, trying to stop him, but he just brushed her off with a teasing laugh.

"No you don't. Historians should be more understanding about someone suffering from curiosity."

"It's just a dress," Melisande protested, too late.

Alex had pulled the silky creation from its nest of tissue paper and was holding it up in front of him, studying the elegant gown. He whistled softly.

"I give Maria top points. You would be absolutely stunning in this dress, Dr. Merrick."

"I don't need an evening dress!"

"Since when did a beautiful woman need an excuse to have a dress like this?"

His words were teasing, and there was a smile on his lips, but something Melisande saw in his eyes as he studied the dress disturbed her. She could imagine what he was thinking—much the same things she had thought when she wore it—and she was anxious to divert his thoughts.

He held it up so that the light caught the lustrous silk, drawing out all the fabric's rich, shifting colors. Abruptly he turned toward Melisande, then held the dress up against her body.

"Top points," he murmured. "It would drive any man mad to see you in a dress like this, Melisande. With your face and figure . . . I can see your hair down, floating about your shoulders, and—"

"Alex!" It was more a plea for deliverance than a protest. His suggestive words and soft voice, the dress, his nearness—they were all wreaking havoc with her self-control.

At her cry Alex started, as though he had been brought back violently from the contemplation of a tantalizing vision.

"You're right," he said with a grin, "it's not good for my blood pressure to let my imagination run away like that."

He took a deep breath, then lowered the dress and stepped back. Though Melisande was struggling to maintain a calm facade, she knew he was aware of her confusion.

"Feijoada?" he asked, casually tossing the dress on top of the open box. "I think we could use a little distraction right now."

The *feijoada* was every bit as good as promised. A sort of stew made of black beans with sausage, pork, and beef, it was served with rice, kale, orange slices, and *farofa,* which Alex explained was made of manioc flour fried with egg and onion.

"It was originally a slave dish, and is usually served as Saturday lunch," he said, "but they serve it regularly here. It's one of the few places I know where you can always get *feijoada,* and it's always good."

"Delicious is a better word," Melisande said as she fished out a bite of sausage.

"Not everyone likes it," Alex admitted. "But then, not everyone seems to adapt to Brazil as quickly as you have. You're not intimidated by Rio's size or its reputation for being unsafe?"

"After living in New York? You must be kidding!"

He laughed. Not for the first time Melisande noted how laughter softened his features.

"You're right. They're both big cities, but . . ."

His words trailed off into nothingness. He sat back for a moment, studying her openly, almost thoughtfully. Melisande carefully mixed some of the food on her plate so she could avoid meeting his eyes. Even when he wasn't holding the green silk dress against her, his gaze was disconcerting.

"Tell me," he said, "how is it possible that a beautiful woman like you has managed to stay single for so many years."

Her head came up. An angry flush warmed her cheeks. "I'm twenty-five! You make it sound as if I'm almost in my dotage!"

"Hardly that." He chuckled. "Though even when you're old you'll be as beautiful as you are now, if in a different way. You have that type of bone structure."

Melisande choked on the food in her mouth. She supposed she ought to be flattered by his thinking she was beautiful, but she wasn't quite ready to discuss her beauty in eventual old age!

"Too hot," she mumbled by way of explanation.

"You still haven't answered my question. At twenty-five many Brazilian women already have one or two children."

"Bully for them. At your age—which must be what? thirty-two? thirty-three?—how many children do Brazilian men generally have? And how many of those are by their wives? I've heard some of them have dozens out of wedlock." She paused. "At least, they do by your age," she added wickedly.

"Ouch!"

"You asked first."

"I wouldn't have if I'd realized you had claws."

"Now you'll know better the next time."

"Cat." His grin took the sting out of his words.

"Meow. Remember, we eat rats."

Alex threw back his head and roared. The echoing laughter drew the attention of everyone in the restaurant.

Melisande couldn't help laughing, too. At times he seemed so arrogant and domineering, yet when he was relaxed and in a good mood, his charm was irresistible.

"Eat your *feijoada,*" he commanded when he was once more in control of himself.

"I will if you'll stop asking personal questions."

"Can I ask impersonal ones?"

Melisande pretended to give his question careful thought.

"Depends on the question," she said at last. "What kinds of impersonal questions?"

"Hmmm." He screwed up his face as though his cogitations were difficult and painful.

"I don't know," he admitted finally. "I can't think of a single impersonal question I want to ask. All I'm interested in is you."

Melisande flushed, startled by the unexpected intensity behind his last words.

"I don't like silly flirting, Alex," she said quietly. "Please don't spoil the evening."

"I didn't mean to sound as if I were flirting."

There was no hint of teasing in his voice. Before Melisande realized what he was doing, he had reached across the table to wrap his hand around hers.

"I really am interested in you, Melisande. Don't you believe me?"

His hand was warm. Though he only held her loosely, his touch melted her resistance. With an effort of will, she slid her hand out from under his and placed it on her lap. She dug her fingers into her napkin, fighting against the tingling heat that sparked across her skin.

"Yes," she said, very low. "I believe you."

The smile that answered her thrilled her like a physical caress. "And are you interested in me?"

She would have sworn that Alex put just the slightest emphasis on the last word.

"Yes," she said.

It would have been impossible to lie, and equally impossible to say more, no matter how inadequate a simple yes was. She almost couldn't hear his reply.

"Then that's all right, isn't it?" he said.

"Eat your *feijoada*," he added, more forcefully. "I can't afford to take out women who don't eat their dinner."

EIGHT

Melisande's work progressed. Though she knew that when she returned to New York she would feel frustrated by the thought of all the research she hadn't had time to do, she was pleased with what she had accomplished so far.

But, she thought with irritation, *if I keep daydreaming I won't get much accomplished from now on.* In spite of her efforts to concentrate, she had found herself, not for the first time that morning, thinking of Alex and not of the work before her.

When he'd brought her home the night before, he couldn't find a place to park, so he'd had to leave her off in front of her apartment building.

Coupled with the regret that he couldn't see her to her door had been relief that there would be no repetition of the kiss that had followed their dinner at the Meridien. Melisande was still too shaken by that experience to be sure she was ready for a repetition quite so soon.

Alex had started to take her in his arms to say good night to her in the car, but the driver of a car behind them began honking his horn because he couldn't pass in the narrow street.

Startled, they'd both jumped, then turned to look back.

"Well, so much for that," Alex had said. He'd brushed a last, quick kiss across her lips, then leaned across her to open her door. "I'm sorry to be so cavalier about saying good night, but I don't want to wake the whole neighborhood, either."

Their smiles and quick good nights had carried regret . . . and Melisande's relief.

"I'll call," he'd said, and then had driven away before the irate driver behind them had had a chance to do more than honk.

Now, seated at the little table that Marta had allocated to her in the archives, Melisande realized she couldn't remember a word of the last few pages she'd read.

She sighed, then closed the book. Perhaps a cup of coffee or a walk would help her get her mind back on track. From experience she knew that the time available for her research would speed past. She couldn't afford to let thoughts of Alex, however tempting, intrude on her work.

"That sounded like a rather heartfelt sigh."

The soft voice so close beside her made Melisande jump.

"Marta! You shouldn't sneak up on a person like that!"

"I was reshelving some books and couldn't help noticing that you seemed to be daydreaming rather than working." The older woman smiled, then winked conspiratorially. "How about some coffee to get the brain cells going again."

"Sounds marvelous. Shall we stay here, or go out?"

They decided to have their coffee in Marta's little cubbyhole. The tiny space was crowded with books

and documents waiting to be catalogued, but it was
air-conditioned. In Rio's hot, humid summer
weather, air-conditioning could make up for a lot
of other discomforts.

"You know," said Melisande as she took a sip of
coffee, "I never thought I would, but I really like
this strong, sweet coffee you drink."

"From what I hear," Marta replied with the air
of someone included in the secret, "our coffee isn't
the only thing you like about Brazil."

Melisande set down her cup with deliberate care.
"What do you mean by that?"

"I mean Alex, of course."

"Alex?"

"You are seeing him, aren't you?"

For a moment all Melisande could do was stare
blankly. She'd said nothing about Alex to Marta.
They'd gone out together only a few times and, with
the exception of the restaurant in the Meridien Hotel, they'd gone only to places where they were un-
likely to meet any of Alex's friends.

"Well . . ." Melisande's blush betrayed her.

"I thought so!" Marta crowed. "Is it serious?"

"I hardly know him! We only met a few days
ago!"

"Sometimes all you need is one meeting."

"Marta! Alex helped me when I was robbed on
the beach. Since then he's taken me to lunch and
out to dinner a couple of times. That's all, and
that's not enough for you to start getting ideas."

"Well, normally I wouldn't," Marta admitted. Her
voice dropped conspiratorially. "But Jorge told me
he saw Alex in a meeting the other day and that

Alex mentioned you several times, that he said he took you up the Corcovado on a workday!"

"Oh, Marta!" Melisande couldn't help breaking into laughter. "You make it sound like something out of the *Arabian Nights!* All he did was take me on a little sightseeing tour and to lunch. There's nothing special in that."

Even though she was trying hard to be offhand and casual, Melisande was aware of a sharp pricking of excitement. If Marta, who had known Alex for years, thought it was significant that he talked about her and took her up the Corcovado, maybe . . .

No, she couldn't let her imagination run loose like that. It would be too easy—and could be far too misleading.

"My dear, Alex *never* lets his little affairs interrupt his work. Never. If he was willing to take some time off to take you up the Corcovado, he's either changed a very great deal, or he's serious. Jorge said he thought, from the way Alex spoke, that he was much more interested than usual. Seriously interested, in fact."

"From what I've heard of the number of girl-friends Alex has gone through over the years, being rather more serious about me doesn't mean a thing."

Melisande spoke flippantly, but all the time she was hoping that she was wrong and Marta was right. Was it so completely impossible to think that Alex might be attracted to her, might even fall in love with her?

"Besides," she continued, "I'm only here a short time; then I have to go back to New York. Alex knows that."

"Historians can work in any place where there are records," Marta snorted, dismissing Melisande's arguments. "If Alex really fell in love with you, he wouldn't let something as unimportant as that stop him."

"He's not in love with me." It took an effort for Melisande to say that.

"He ought to be." The emphatic statement made Melisande sit up suddenly in surprise. "It's about time he forgot all those tramps who hurt him when he was younger, the women who chased him for his money and his position, who thought his good looks and charm were simply sweet frosting on a very rich cake."

Marta set her coffee cup down so hard the saucer rattled under it. "He's old enough now to know when a woman can be trusted not to be interested in him just because he's rich. He *needs* a woman in his life, and you would be the perfect complement to him, Melisande."

Melisande could only stare.

"Don't look so surprised. You're intelligent, kind, and sweet. You're also beautiful. Alex is lonely and ready to settle down. He'd know it, too, if he were only willing to be honest with himself. Oh, he still goes around with this chip on his shoulder about women who are after his money, but if you want my opinion, I think it's just because he's waited so long to get married that now he's afraid even to consider it."

Marta's forthright words left Melisande so dazed that she spent the rest of the morning staring blindly at her books without reading them.

Could Marta be right? Melisande wondered. And

even if Alex were interested in something more than just a pleasant friendship, was *she* ready to deal with anything more intense?

She was, she admitted to herself, powerfully attracted to Alex, both physically and emotionally. He was easy to be with, fun to talk to, and he had the power to stir her as no other man had ever done. But was she really ready to face all the risks and commitments that falling in love entailed?

Her life was pleasant, productive, and interesting. Even in the short time she'd known him, Alex had managed to disrupt that carefully constructed order. Falling in love—

No, she was better off not thinking about it. He wasn't falling in love with her. She didn't want to fall in love with him. She would enjoy his company while she was here in Brazil, and then she would happily go back to teaching at the university. That was absolutely the most sensible approach to the whole affair.

But just when she had managed to convince herself, Melisande would remember the way his arms felt around her, the way his kisses burned her lips, and the way her body responded to his. Even the memory of his embraces was enough to make her flush, then shift uncomfortably with the heat that rushed through her.

The handful of precious and semiprecious gems scattered across the velvet cloth glittered and sparked fire in the light from the desk lamp, yet Alex took no pleasure from their beauty. Today they had as much appeal as a pebble on Ipanema beach.

Less, since there was always the chance he'd run into Melisande Merrick if he went for a walk on the beach.

The thought irritated him even more, making him frown at the uncooperative bits of rock. He had agreed to design a fantasy brooch for an old friend, but inspiration eluded him. When the hundredth sketch had ended up a crumpled wad of paper in the trash can, along with the ninety-nine that had preceeded it, he'd tried a trick that had often worked for him in the past—he'd selected a number of interestingly shaped and colored stones from the company safe, then laid them out on the velvet in the hope that the casual array might tweak an idea or two in his recalcitrant brain.

The trick wasn't working today.

Nothing was working except his own overheated imagination, and it refused to imagine anything except a certain brown-haired, green-eyed historian.

He nudged a watermelon tourmaline, studying the subtle shadings of color at either end and the abrupt transition from pink to green in the middle that gave the stone its name.

Not a particularly valuable stone, even at its best, but he'd always liked it. It was one of Mother Nature's jokes, a playful piece that seemed to say that nothing, not even this, should be taken seriously. The colors of it, so clear and sharp, always made him think of blue skies and bright sun, and somehow when he worked with it, he felt happy. Sometimes it even made him laugh for no reason at all, just because he liked it, and it was fun. Today, nothing was making him laugh, not even the tourmaline.

The diamonds were worse.

Alex studied the small pile of them heaped on the velvet like a gaudy miniature mountain. The stones were of varying sizes, clarity, and quality, but they were alike in that they took the light and twisted it and gave it back brighter than before. Yet despite the white fire within them, they seemed cold and unfriendly, inhuman in their icy purity.

He'd never particularly cared for diamonds, no matter how valuable they were. He preferred color and warmth, and diamonds had neither, not even the yellow and blue ones. They were hard and unforgiving stones. He used them in his designs because their light emphasized the color of the emeralds and rubies and sapphires that he preferred. He used them because he had to, because customers wanted diamonds, even if something softer and more colorful might have suited them more.

Most jewelers thought in terms of color and size and whether or not the gem and the jewelry would suit the wearer. Though Alex had seldom talked about it, he'd always thought of gems in terms of people, in terms of emotion and soul. He still remembered a long-ago argument with his father, who had been exasperated by his son's fanciful notions. Alex had lost that argument and he'd kept his thoughts to himself ever since, but that didn't mean he'd changed his mind on the subject.

He dragged his finger through the collected gems, toppling the diamond mountain, disordering the already haphazard arrangement. The gems sparked and winked with the movement, vivid against the dark cloth.

A yellow topaz was earthy, unpretentious, warm.

A blue topaz was for dreamers, someone just a little . . . ethereal. Opals were for gentle souls, peridots for practical ones, diamonds for the hard-edged, ambitious types. Rubies, on the other hand, were for dark, driven people while sapphires were for intense, artistic individuals.

But which was Melisande's stone?

His hand froze, suspended over the velvet. He studied the gems scattered in front of him.

He hadn't meant to think of her. He had, in fact, been trying all morning to push her out of his thoughts so he could focus on his work. To no avail. She had a way of sneaking in sideways, of slipping under his guard and evading his defenses like a clever jewel thief bent on plundering his treasures.

Alex studied the gems scattered on the velvet. Diamonds, tourmalines, topazes, opals, amethysts, sapphires, peridots, emeralds, rubies, aquamarines—

Emeralds.

He frowned, then picked up the largest of the three emeralds that lay on the velvet.

Melisande was emeralds. Deep, green, vivid emeralds. Soft and warm and bright. Alive with a fire that warmed instead of burned.

He brought the gem closer to the desk lamp, holding it between thumb and forefinger and turning it gently so it caught the light. It was a beautiful stone, small, yet with the deep, rich green color of the very finest emeralds. He held it closer to the light and leaned closer, studying it.

The secret of emeralds was that, despite their beauty, they were almost always flawed. The flaws, sometimes called gardens, depending on their nature, could actually add to the value of the stones, but they were almost always there.

Almost always.

Alex took a deep breath, then carefully set the emerald down with its mates.

He had to remember that. *Had* to.

Even the most beautiful emeralds had flaws.

Melisande returned home that evening, physically tired, emotionally exhausted, and very, very frustrated that she'd been unable to push thoughts of Alex out of her mind and concentrate on her work. Yet despite her weariness, she couldn't repress the eagerness rising within her. She would be seeing him soon.

She knew it wasn't wise to focus so much energy and thought on this one man, or on any man for that matter. Not when she had work to do and little time in which to do it. Not when she knew she would be leaving Brazil in a few months and might never return. Not when she knew Alex wasn't serious about her—would *never* be serious about her—and she risked heartbreak if she let herself become serious about him.

Sensible, rational reservations, and not one of them could dampen her enthusiasm or her growing excitement at the prospect of being with him again, even if only for a few short hours.

Senhora Amado met her at the door with the announcement that Senhor Alex had called. Though her Portuguese was still too weak for her to be sure, Melisande thought that the message was that he was tied up with work and would not be able to see her that evening as they had planned. She wasn't sure whether she was more disappointed or relieved.

A few hours later, hunched over the stacks of notes at the long library table in the apartment, Melisande had to admit that disappointment was eating at her and keeping her from concentrating.

She threw down her pen in disgust. A whole day wasted. A day that she could have—*should* have— spent digging into her research, but that she'd frittered away with foolish daydreams about a man she scarcely knew.

Acknowledging defeat, at least for that day, she straightened her notes and went to bed, vowing that her dreams, at least, would be free of one Alex Robeson.

Whether they were or not, she didn't know because she couldn't remember them when she awoke. It took a real effort of will, but she managed to get some work done the following morning. She wasn't sorry when noon came and she could escape, however. She had arranged to meet Maria for lunch. The lively redhead would be sure to have so many things to talk about that she wouldn't have time to think about Alex.

It was, therefore, a shock to find her friend seated at a table for four with her husband on one side and Alex on the other.

Melisande's stride faltered for an instant. Beside the petite redhead and the slim, blond banker, Alex looked even more overwhelmingly masculine than usual. To her chagrin, Melisande felt a flush creeping up her cheeks. Her stomach twisted, but not with pain.

"Isn't this nice?" Maria crowed. "I talked Stephen

into getting out of his stuffy bank, and he brought Alex along."

"I had a meeting with Stephen," Alex added apologetically, rising to hold Melisande's chair for her. "I hope you don't mind."

"No, not at all. I'm delighted. How are you, Stephen?"

The task of greeting her friends and getting settled in her chair gave Melisande the time she needed to regain control of herself. But even though she was calmer, she was intensely aware of the dark man beside her. She hoped no one noticed that she was avoiding looking directly at him.

Despite her initial shock, Melisande found the lunch went off very pleasantly. The presence of Maria and Stephen made it impossible for her to concentrate on Alex or on her reactions to him. And with the lively discussion the others maintained, her occasional moments of not speaking were not noticed.

Over coffee afterward, Stephen said, "I almost forgot, Melisande! Our little yacht's out of dry dock and floating again. The workmen promise it won't sink for a least a few more days. Maria and I were going to call you and see if you were interested in going for a sail."

Melisande's eyes lit up with enthusiasm. Before she could say anything, Stephen grinned and said, "I can see you're interested. And if you have no objection, we can even invite this oversized fellow along. He can bail if necessary."

"I've no objection to Alex coming," she said. "Is he any good at bailing?"

With an effort, Melisande repressed the urge to

grab Alex's hand. She could only hope the glance she threw him didn't reveal any more of her delight that he was to be included than was politely safe.

"I'm more accustomed to swabbing the decks," Alex said doubtfully, "but my talents are varied. If it really ended up being necessary, I could probably manage to bail, too."

His eyes, when he met Melisande's glance, were twinkling appealingly.

"Forget the bailing," said Maria, grinning. "You're going to be Melisande's and my galley slave!"

Alex leered wickedly. "Is that a promise?"

Melisande laughed to cover her own eagerness.

"Would Sunday be all right?" Stephen asked, ignoring the interruption.

They managed to work out times and meeting places before Stephen said regretfully that he had to return to work. As they all rose to say good-bye, Melisande wondered if she'd made a mistake in accepting the invitation. Was it really wise to spend more time with Alex? Thoughts of him were already taking up her working time. A sailing trip, even with friends, sounded rather dangerously romantic.

NINE

Melisande returned from her run on Sunday morning energized by the exercise and looking forward to the promised sail. Her earlier doubts had eased when she had reminded herself that she wouldn't be alone with Alex. They would be chaperoned—though that really wasn't the right word for it, of course—by Stephen and Maria. And they were, after all, only going to be out for an afternoon's sail. What could be risky about that?

Going up in the elevator she pulled off her T-shirt dress and rolled it, along with her cheap plastic sandals, in the towel she carried. Because of the sand that invariably clung to her after her swim she had developed the habit of pulling all but her swimsuit off in the elevator in order to avoid tracking up the apartment's carpets.

Now she studied her reflection in the elevator's mirror, pleased with what she saw. She had always been trim and fit, but the regular morning exercise had firmed and shaped her curves to the point that she had ventured to buy one of the brightly colored and, to her eyes, daring swimsuits that were available in Rio. This one consisted of two bands of cloth, one black and one brilliant blue, that wrapped around to cover, barely, all the strategic points, while managing to accent her small waist and curving hips.

It was far more daring than her other suits, and she had decided to buy it only when the sales clerk had pointed out that, by Rio's standards, it was conservative.

Since Melisande had seen some suits that consisted of little more than a couple of pieces of string and almost nonexistent scraps of fabric, she couldn't argue the point. She had to admit, she did feel rather daring with her firmer figure and golden tan. And who that she knew would see her on the beach, anyway?

She took one last glance in the mirror when the elevator doors opened, then skipped across the foyer to ring the bell by the front door. After the robbery on the beach, she had been careful to take nothing of value with her in the mornings. Senhora Amado would let her into the apartment.

Since Melisande was expecting to see the housekeeper's round, pleasant face when the door opened, it came as a shock that Alex greeted her instead. She was vaguely aware that he was dressed in white slacks and a knit shirt that beautifully set off the powerful lines of his body, but her attention was caught by the expression in his dark eyes as he became aware of her own state of dress.

As his gaze, first startled, then frankly admiring, ran down the length of her body to her bare feet, Melisande could feel her cheeks flaming in embarrassment.

"I, uh, take off my beach dress and things so I don't track sand in the house," she stammered.

"So I see. Don't you want to come in?"

He stepped aside to let her pass. As Melisande slipped by him, she had a strong suspicion his grin was as much for her embarrassment as for her attire.

"However," he continued, "with such a conservative suit I don't imagine you really need a beach dress. At least, not in Rio."

She couldn't see his face because he had turned to shut the door, but the amusement in his voice was clear.

"Well, I wasn't expecting you for another two hours. If I'd known you were going to come early—"

He interrupted her. "I hope you wouldn't have changed on my account." He grinned. "You look stunning in that suit. But maybe you'll want to change before I explain why I arrived early. Senhora Amado has set out what she tells me is your usual breakfast of fruit and coffee. I was about to get a cup for myself, so I'm in no hurry. No hurry whatsoever."

Melisande blinked, dazed by the warmth and approval that shone so clearly in his eyes.

"Senhora Amado makes cood coffee," she said, then blushed at the slightly breathless note in her voice. His gaze was enough to steal the air from her lungs and set her heart pounding.

"At any rate"—his eyes twinkled appreciatively as he studied the effect of the skimpy suit—"it shouldn't take you long to slip out of that thing."

Melisande started to voice a retort, but she stifled it when a flush of embarrassment threatened to embarrass her more. She settled for a growl of frustration and dashed down the hall to the safety of her room.

When she reappeared a little while later, she was dressed in a neat pair of full, white boating shorts that came to the middle of her thighs and a demure white, short-sleeved knit top similar to the one Alex wore. Her hair, still damp, was up in its usual bun, suitable for the tennis cap she carried in her bag.

She found Alex in the dining room, sipping on a cup of coffee and studying the morning newspapers. A place had been set for her, with platters of tropical fruits and a variety of breads for her to choose from. She picked up her cup and walked past Alex to fill it from the coffeepot on the side board, deliberately ignoring the amused expression on his face as she passed.

"Very nice. Would you mind if I said I preferred your first outfit?"

"You wouldn't have seen it if you hadn't been so rudely early," said Melisande as she returned to her chair.

She was relieved that no betraying blush threatened the brave front she was putting up. As she had dressed she had realized, to her chagrin, that she had been as much delighted as embarrassed that Alex had seen her in her new swimsuit, and that he had approved. If she wasn't careful, she was liable to start taking his flirtatious teasing seriously. Too seriously.

A too-juicy papaya provided the perfect distraction. She couldn't yet risk looking directly at the disturbing man on the other side of the breakfast table. There was something surprisingly intimate in having him share breakfast with her, dressed in sporting clothes that only accented his undeniable masculinity and calmly reading the papers as though they were both accustomed to such a domestic routine.

Her ruse failed, however, for a chuckle from across the table brought her gaze up to meet his before she could think about it.

"Was I *that* obvious?" he asked.

Melisande, a slice of papaya halfway to her mouth, stared at him.

"I didn't mean to embarrass you, you know," he said gently. "If I did, I apologize."

He chuckled. "It was just the shock of seeing you suddenly appear on the doorstep in the role of knockout bathing beauty that got to me."

"Well . . . Uh . . ." She swallowed uncomfortably. Her gaze dropped to the papaya on her fork.

Rather than struggle to find something intelligent to say, she ate the papaya, then followed it with a too-large bite of bread. Chewing at least kept her mouth busy and out of trouble.

"I arrived so early," he said, "because I thought you might be interested in going to the Ipanema Art Fair. Though you might have heard of it as the Hippie Fair. Do you know it?"

Melisande ignored the happy thrill of excitement that suddenly ran through her and nodded instead. Her mouth was still far too full for her to talk.

"You've been?" His gaze dropped to her mouth.

She shook her head, then hastily swallowed the last of the bread and dabbed at her mouth with her napkin. "I've been once, just after I arrived. It's not so far from here, and I always meant to go back but never did. I'd love to go with you. Thank you."

Alex wrenched his gaze from her lips. "Great," he said, perhaps a shade too heartily. "I haven't been in ages, and this seemed a perfect opportunity. We can go whenever you're ready. For convenience I had my driver bring me; we can just tell him to pick us up there."

They walked to the fair, which was located in an open plaza only a block from Ipanema beach. It was alive with color and movement.

Booths displaying handmade jewelry, embroidered clothes, leather goods, straw baskets, hand-blown glass ornaments, whimsical creations for a home or office, and a bewildering variety of unclassifiable miscellany jammed the plaza's walks. Artists had set up racks and easels to show their paintings, sculptors mounted their pieces on boxes and portable shelves, and balloon and toy sellers roamed about selling their wares. Tourists, families out for the morning, and young people curious to see what was new strolled about and browsed among the stalls.

Attracted by a booth displaying brightly colored, fanciful animals made of clay, Melisande left Alex to pore over a collection of old prints and maps. She hadn't meant to buy anything, but one item made her laugh, then dive in her purse for the money to pay for it. A moment later, she was back at Alex's side, almost quivering with mingled triumph and amusement . . . and just a touch of nervousness at her boldness.

Alex grinned down at her. "I just realized you escaped and was wondering how I was going to find you. By the look on your face you've been up to something. Do I dare want to know about it?"

"I've bought you a present," said Melisande, grinning in return and stretching out her closed fists toward him. "If you can guess which hand it's in, you can have it."

"Tease. And what if I don't guess? Can I take it by force?"

"Of course not," said Melisande in mock indignation. "But I might let you have it, anyway. Guess."

After a show of careful consideration Alex pointed to her right hand.

Melisande stamped her foot and protested, "You guessed!"

"Well, I had a fifty-fifty chance, and besides, your left hand was clenched tight, and the right one was more open. Do I get to see my prize?"

"All right, Sherlock."

With a giggle Melisande opened her hand to display a small, bright green plaster frog nestled in her palm. It was hung from a thin leather cord to make a necklace of the kind worn by young girls.

"A frog?"

"A tree frog. I thought it might be more comfortable hung from your neck than stuck down the back of your shirt."

Melisande couldn't help laughing at the quizzical expression that crossed Alex's face before he, too, burst out laughing.

"That wretch Maria has been telling tales out of school. Well, you'll have to put it on me. I'm not accustomed to wearing necklaces."

He smiled at her and Melisande, meeting his dark eyes so close above her now, caught her breath at the sudden warmth that flowed through her.

It seemed an endless moment before she could say lightly, "You'll have to bend down, then. You're only about two feet taller than I am."

"A gross exaggeration," he protested. "I'm not an inch over six-one, and you're five-seven if you're an inch."

"Five-eight," she said firmly, "and you're still too tall. Turn around and bend down."

It would, she thought, *be less disturbing if I didn't have to look at him until I could regain my self-control.* When she'd picked up the little clay frog, she'd thought it would be a good joke to give it to him, but now she wondered if the joke wasn't on her. In spite of all the time they had spent together he still could disturb her with a simple smile, and this close—

She cut off the thought before she lost her nerve completely.

Alex did as he was bid, but Melisande found his nearness no less disconcerting just because she could not see his face. Her fingers trembled slightly as she reached around him to pull the leather cord in place, and she fumbled with the clasp. She almost dropped the cord when her fingertips grazed the warm skin at the back of his neck, and the faint smell of his aftershave, mixed with the clean, male smell of his skin, did not help.

Because of her own confusion, Melisande scarcely noticed Alex's sudden tenseness, and she could only be grateful that he took a long moment, after she succeeded in fastening the cord, before he turned to face her.

"I'm sure it looks great," he said lightly, trying in vain to peer under his own chin, "but I hope none of my stockholders see me. They'll wonder why I didn't do it in gold and emeralds."

"Tell them you covered up the real jewels so no

one would steal them. It's an ancient ruse to disguise valuables and foil robbers, you know." Her own voice was equally light.

"The perfect excuse," Alex agreed. His voice seemed oddly tight.

Melisande glanced at the little frog where it lay against the smooth, tanned skin at the base of his throat and, as quickly, looked away again. It wouldn't do to let her thoughts stray past the opening of the knit shirt he wore—she was already too aware of the powerful line of shoulder and chest it showed so clearly beneath its soft fabric.

"I see my driver over there," Alex said, interrupting her dangerous train of thought. "Shall we go on to the harbor?"

Maria and Stephen Sebastian shouted an enthusiastic welcome from the graceful, single-masted, white boat that was moored beside the pier. Alex helped Melisande down the steps, and Stephen stretched out a hand to help her jump over the rail and onto the deck.

"I was beginning to wonder if we would ever get you out, Alex," Maria teased. "I've lost track of the number of times we've invited you." Perched as she was on the cabin roof, she could look down at her tall friend and clearly meant to make use of her advantage.

"I didn't want you to start taking me for granted, Red." Alex grinned up at the pert redhead above him.

She pulled off her wide-brimmed straw hat and swung it at him playfully.

"You know I don't let anyone call me Red. And where," she demanded suddenly, "did you get that ridiculous little frog?"

Alex dodged gracefully out of Maria's reach. "Don't call it ridiculous, Red, or you'll hurt Melisande's feelings. She bought it for me at the Ipanema fair this morning. It seems you've been ratting on me, and she decided to rub it in."

"And you got him to wear it?" Maria looked at Melisande in awe. "How did you ever do that?"

Melisande, accepting a drink Stephen offered her, exchanged a quick, smiling glance with Alex before turning back to Maria.

"I never tell my secrets," she said haughtily. Then she giggled. "I think the whole idea was so silly, he couldn't think of anything to say fast enough."

She looked up as Alex, drink in hand, came to stand beside her, a wide grin on his face.

"I didn't do anything because you attacked me when I wasn't looking. I didn't have a chance to defend myself. Get your facts straight, woman." He glared at her in mock ferocity.

Maria, startled, glanced quickly at Alex, who stood looking down at Melisande, then more thoughtfully at Melisande's upturned face. She gave her husband a questioning look and was met by an expression of puzzled interest.

Stephen, one eyebrow cocked in amused speculation, threw one last, brief look to where Melisande and Alex still stood, frozen, then casually asked the world at large, "Everybody ready to go?"

He couldn't help but notice the way the two started as they came back to awareness of their surroundings. He knew his wife would have seen, too, and wondered what she thought of it.

Melisande quickly moved away from Alex and toward Stephen.

"Of course we're ready to go," she said gaily. "What can I do?"

She was more shaken by that brief, intense exchange of glances than she cared to admit and was anxious to find a distraction.

"Nothing," said Stephen firmly. "With Alex to serve as deckhand, you and Maria can loll about and enjoy the ride. You're going to find that Guanabara Bay is one of the most beautiful in the world. Take advantage of us poor, overworked males, at least this once."

Melisande couldn't help but laugh at the exaggerated look of long-suffering tolerance on Stephen's face or at his wife's good-natured, derisory catcalls from the cabin roof.

Once they started, Melisande found Stephen had not exaggerated in praising the beautiful bay that was one of Rio's chief attractions. The modern city, strung out along the vast beaches, glowed in the bright sun against a backdrop of tall, hazy-blue mountains. The many small islands which dotted the vast bay floated in a sea of sapphire blue that sparkled like flashing diamonds in the reflected sunlight. A cool sea breeze relieved the clinging humidity as spray flung up from the bow misted refreshingly on their skin.

The two women were comfortably settled on the cushioned seats in the well behind the cabin. A table in the center of the well, which they would use for lunch, divided them. They were at liberty to enjoy the beauty around them while the men steered or moved about, adjusting the sails.

Far more times than she would have liked, Melisande found her gaze drifting to Alex. He moved so easily around the tilting deck, obviously at home on a sailing boat. As he bent to pull a rope taut or shifted to follow the movement of the boat as it cut through the waves, she could see the muscles in his arms and back and legs move under his clothing. The wind tossed his dark hair into an appealing tangle, and his features became younger, more relaxed.

Often, when she glanced toward him, she would find his gaze already upon her. Their eyes would meet, sometimes only for an instant, and he would smile. The smile and the warmth in his dark eyes were like an electric shock, jumping the distance separating them and flashing through her as if he were a bolt of lightning and she a lightning rod.

Much of the time Alex was able to join her and Maria. He would settle comfortably on one of the cushioned seats, sometimes joining their conversation, sometimes content just to listen. Though Melisande tried, she could not repress the eager tension that coursed through her at his nearness. The well was small, capable of seating no more than six people, and Alex was a big man. His presence overflowed the small space, wrapping around her inescapably.

Melisande, intensely aware of Alex, never noticed Maria's thoughtful, speculative glances. She would have been extremely embarrassed had she had any idea of the thoughts running through her friend's mind.

TEN

The morning passed quickly, but delightfully. Only a sudden realization that she was hungry made Melisande agree to mooring near one of the small, palm-covered islands when Stephen finally suggested they stop for lunch.

Once they were anchored she helped Maria lay out a tempting lunch, to be accompanied by chilled white wine, while the men strung a nylon canvas to provide some protective shade against the strong tropical sun.

She sighed happily as she settled on one of the bright blue deck cushions and gazed about her, conscious of a sense of total contentment. When she caught Alex watching her she couldn't help laughing out loud.

"You're extremely cheerful, madam," he said, meeting her happy smile with a wide, sympathetic smile of his own.

"It's just so *beautiful*," she said, laughing again. "On a wonderful day like this, with the company of good friends and in such a spectacular setting, how could someone *not* be happy?"

"That's what you need to be happy?" he asked, gesturing out at the distant mountains. "Just this?"

"Well," she said, cocking her head meditatively

while she gazed past him at the shimmering vista of sun, sea, and mountain, "I also have my work. And," she added, her eyes twinkling, "I wouldn't mind some of that chicken Maria just set out on the table."

"A wise choice," said Stephen approvingly as he drew the cork out of a well-chilled bottle of wine. "And while you're at it, how about some of this?" He carefully filled four wineglasses then passed them around as they seated themselves at the sunken deck table in the well.

They touched glasses, and as Melisande started to take a sip of the tantalizingly cold wine, she stopped and asked impulsively, "May I make a toast?"

With Stephen's smiling approval, Melisande lifted her glass and said simply, "To good friends."

Her eyes met Maria's laughing glance, then Stephen's, and slid on to lock with Alex's suddenly intent gaze. For a moment she remained caught by those dark brown eyes, unaware of the look that was exchanged between Maria and Stephen. Then she tentatively lifted her glass to touch Alex's.

"To good friends," he agreed softly.

The food proved to be every bit as delicious as it looked, and disappeared faster than Melisande would have believed possible. When she at last collapsed against the cushion behind her there was little left for her to choose from even if she had wanted more.

"I didn't think it was possible to eat so much," groaned Maria, stretching out contentedly. "I'm glad you guys are going to clean up."

Prone, she couldn't dodge the well-aimed cushion her husband threw at her.

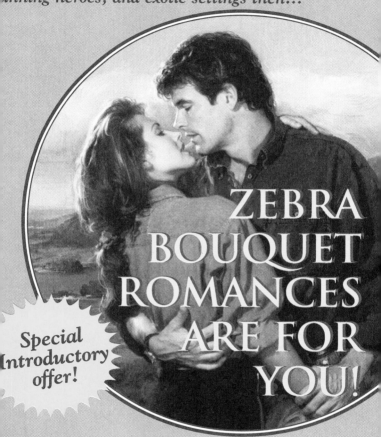

The publishers of Zebra Bouquet are making this special offer to lovers of contemporary romances to introduce this exciting new line of romance novels. Zebra's Bouquet Romances have been praised by critics and authors alike as being of the highest quality and best written romantic fiction available today.

Each full-length novel has been written by authors you know and love as well as by up-and-coming writers that you'll only find with Zebra Bouquet. We'll bring you the newest novels by world famous authors like Vanessa Grant, Judy Gill, Ann Josephson and award winning Suzanne Barrett and Leigh Greenwood to name just a few. Zebra Bouquet's editors have selected only the very best and highest quality for publication under the Bouquet banner.

You'll be treated to glamorous settings from Carnavale in Rio, the moneyed high-powered offices of New York's Wall Street, the rugged north coast of British Columbia, the mountains of North Carolina, all the way to the bull rings of Spain. Bouquet Romances use these settings to spin tales of star-crossed lovers caught in "nail biting" dilemmas that are sure to captivate you. These stories will keep you on the edge of your seat to the very happy end.

4 FREE NOVELS As a way to introduce you to these terrific romances, the publishers of Bouquet are offering Zebra Romance readers Four Free Bouquet novels. They are yours for the asking with no obligation to buy a single book. Read them at your leisure. We are sure that after you've read these introductory books you'll want more! (If you do not wish to receive any further Bouquet novels, simply write "cancel" on the invoice and return to us within 10 days.)

SAVE 20% WITH HOME DELIVERY

Each month you'll receive four just published Bouquet Romances. We'll ship them to you as soon as they are printed (you may even get them before the bookstores). You'll have 10 days to preview these exciting novels for Free. If you decide to keep them, you'll be billed the special preferred home subscription price of just $3.20 per book; a total of just $12.80 — that's a savings of 20% off the publishers price. If for any reason you are not satisfied simply return the novels for full credit, no questions asked. You'll never have to purchase a minimum number of books and you may cancel your subscription at any time.

BOUQUET ROMANCE
120 Brighton Road
P.O. BOX 5214
Clifton, New Jersey 07015-5214

AFFIX
STAMP
HERE

"Galley wenches are lucky they get fed," Stephen laughingly warned her. "They'd better not think of trying to get out of any work on top of it all!"

From her comfortable seat at one end of the table Melisande watched the ensuing friendly tussle between Stephen and Maria. What these two friends had, she thought, was not just a marriage, but a deep and abiding friendship that strengthened the love they shared. Would she ever find such friendship? she wondered. Would she ever find such love?

A chuckle from beside her brought her out of her reverie with a start. She turned to see Alex, at the other end of the long cushion, watching his friends.

He glanced over at her, the edges of his eyes crinkled with laughter. His long body leaned negligently against the cushions, one leg up, arms outstretched on either side, more relaxed and at ease than she had ever seen him. All she had to do, she realized, was to stretch out a hand to touch his where it lay on the seat back close to her. She dropped her hand into her lap, suddenly, intensely aware of his nearness.

"I don't think Maria will ever grow up," he said softly, shaking his head in amusement. "And it would be a tragedy if she did. Without her, Stephen would be too serious. And he gives her the stability she needs."

"They have a very special marriage," agreed Melisande, also softly. "What they have is what marriage should be about."

She was looking at her friends, not at him, but she was suddenly aware of an abrupt change in his manner. However, when she looked over at him, he sat up to throw a cushion at Maria, who was pummeling her hapless husband. Melisande couldn't see his face.

"Hey, you two!" Alex warned with mock sternness. "Remember you're our hosts! Maria, don't be so mean to poor Stephen. You know he can't stand pain!"

Maria sat up abruptly, her bright red hair tousled appealingly, and grinned. "I *have* to keep him in line," she protested. "Otherwise he behaves terribly."

"Keep me in line, will you!" Stephen's head suddenly popped up on the other side of the table. "Try it and I'll run away with Melisande. She'd be kind to me, at least. Wouldn't you, Melisande?"

Melisande couldn't help bursting into laughter at the comic appeal on Stephen's handsome, slender face. "Of course I would. Where shall we run away to?"

"The South Seas," was the only suggestion Stephen managed to get out before he was laughingly forced to dodge another cushion.

"You promised to take me there, you beast!" Maria said between giggles. "I'll run away with Alex, then. You'll see."

"Not with me, you won't," protested Alex with a grin, rising to his feet with agile grace. "I'd never be able to live with a termagant like you. I'm going to rescue the wine and Melisande, and then retire to a safe distance from the Sebastian family squabbles."

Laughing, he reached a hand to help Melisande rise. Glancing up at him, she could detect no trace in his face of the tension she thought she had sensed a few moments before. She accepted his hand with an answering laugh and, once on her feet, reached for their wineglasses.

"Stephen, they're stealing the wine!"

The threat was sufficient to bring both Sebastians, wineglasses in hand and suitably subdued, to join them. The four of them settled at the stern and dangled their legs over the side, watching the late afternoon light gradually changing the texture and color of the land and sea around them.

"Besides," Maria continued once they were comfortably seated, "you can't run off to the South Seas. Carnaval is only a little more than a week away, and I have such wonderful costumes for Stephen and me. I couldn't possibly go anywhere until after Carnaval, and I won't let Stephen go, either. It would spoil all my plans."

Carnaval was the traditional celebration before the sacrifices and fasting of Lent began, and Rio's Carnaval was world famous for its exotic spectacle, brilliant costumes, wild parties, and beautiful women. Melisande had planned to explore the street festivals that jammed Rio's boulevards during the day, but so far she had received no invitations to any of the evening parties.

It would have been fun, she knew, to attend the famous Carnaval balls dressed in one of the beautiful, glittering costumes for which they were famous, but tickets were extremely expensive and hard to come by. In addition, she didn't have a costume and she would need an escort, which she didn't have, either.

"What are your costumes?" asked Melisande with sudden interest.

"I can't tell you. They're a surprise. Even Stephen doesn't know." Maria's bright eyes twinkled mischievously.

"Which probably means I am going to be extremely embarrassed to be seen in it," moaned Stephen, taking a fortifying drink of wine. "My only consolation will be that we'll be on Sugar Loaf and there will be so many other people in crazy costumes no one will ever know the difference."

"You're going to the ball on Sugar Loaf? That would be wonderful!" breathed Melisande, her eyes shining.

Sugar Loaf is the mountain of rock that resembles the "loaves" of sugar sold during colonial times. It soars several hundred feet above Rio's beaches and is reached by cable car. During Carnaval it is the site of one of the most exotic and famous of Rio's Carnaval balls.

Maria straightened suddenly, almost bouncing in excitement.

"Stephen! Melisande and Alex can use the Bakers' tickets!"

"Of course!" said Stephen, suddenly as animated as his wife. "Perfect!"

Seeing the puzzlement on Melisande's and Alex's faces, he explained. "We got two tickets for some friends of ours from the States, but at the last minute they found they couldn't come. We were going to sell them because everyone else we knew already had plans. Why don't you two come with us? It would be much more fun to go with someone we know."

Melisande glowed at the thought, then sobered as another thought struck her.

"I have no costume, I'm afraid, and there's not enough time to make one." She tried to keep the disappointment from her face. "And I'm sure Alex has plans. Thank you for inviting me, though."

No one said anything for a moment, but Maria studied Melisande's face anxiously.

"Well, Alex, as it happens, doesn't have plans and would very much like to go with Melisande."

Alex's voice was carefully casual, but when Melisande glanced up at him in stunned surprise, the expression on his face was oddly quizzical. Had it been anyone else, she would have said it was almost timid.

He smiled gently down at her.

"I have a costume I could wear, and you really shouldn't pass up the chance to go to one of Rio's biggest Carnaval balls."

He looked toward Maria.

"Isn't there any way we can get Melisande a costume? Through one of the big samba schools, maybe, or a friend who might have a costume she won't be using?"

In a daze, Melisande listened to the three of them discussing possible ways of obtaining a suitable costume. Her thoughts whirled. She felt like a teenager who had just been unexpectedly asked to the senior prom by the captain of the football team: excited and not quite sure it was really true.

Even after everyone had agreed on Maria's plan to get a costume and they had cleaned up the luncheon things, weighed anchor, and were sailing back in the glowing twilight, Melisande wasn't quite convinced of the reality of it all. She shared in the quiet conversation and reveled in the beauty that surrounded them, but her mind kept dancing around one thought: she was going to the Sugar Loaf Ball, and she was going with Alex.

The following days passed almost too quickly for Melisande to be able to distinguish one from another. She maintained her grueling schedule of long hours in the archives, but now many of her evenings were spent with Alex.

Together they roamed the city, exploring neighborhoods that tourists seldom saw. On occasion they took buses almost at random, spending hours watching people passing by.

To Melisande, their wanderings offered an incomparable opportunity to learn more about this complex, fascinating city. Before, her time had been spent exploring the area around Ipanema and Copacabana, or around the archives and libraries she visited regularly. Now she was beginning to see other areas hidden away behind the hills around which Rio was built, places she'd never realized existed.

While her historian's mind delighted in what she saw and learned, with each outing, each new adventure, her woman's heart blossomed with the growing certainty that she was falling in love with Alex Robeson.

It wasn't just that he was overwhelmingly masculine and undeniably attractive. And it certainly had nothing to do with his wealth, for Melisande consciously avoided mentioning his business or accepting his invitations to dine at some of Rio's more exclusive, and extraordinarily expensive, restaurants.

Physical attraction, she knew, had something to do with her feelings toward Alex. She had only to be with him to feel her body responding to his nearness. And, as amazing as it sometimes seemed to her, she knew that he felt the same.

A simple touch, a passing glance, could set her heart racing. Just the sight of his hair, disordered by a passing breeze, was enough to start a slow curl of warmth in the pit of her stomach or to make her muscles tingle and her breath catch unevenly.

When he left her at the door of her apartment, Melisande sometimes found herself rushing to the mirror to assure herself that his kisses hadn't left a brand upon her skin. It was increasingly a struggle for her to stop before their lovemaking progressed too far. And it was, she knew, no easier for Alex.

But mere physical attraction wasn't enough to explain the utter contentment she felt in his presence or the eagerness with which she looked forward to being with him.

To say there was a meeting of the minds between them was to simplify the matter too much. They were interested in many of the same things, intrigued by ideas, moved by the life they saw around them, eager to learn more and see more of what the world had to offer. When silence fell between them, it was comfortably companionable rather than strained. When they talked, and they could talk for hours, they delighted in discussing almost anything that came to mind.

It was exciting, and intriguing, to find, for the first time in her life, a man who could laugh at the same things she did, and understand her, even when she found it difficult to explain herself.

Melisande suspected that the shared exploration was, for Alex, an escape from the pressures of his job and his social position. Occasionally, such as when passersby were rude or too presumptuous, or people on the buses pushed too hard, he would stiffen and his chin would tilt to an arrogant angle. But Melisande had found she needed only to touch his arm or murmur a soft word of warning for him to relax and remember where they were.

Sometimes he said things that made her wonder what kind of childhood he'd had. He spoke of Maria with affection, and recounted some of the exploits he and his friends had indulged in as schoolchildren, but from some of his comments Melisande suspected that he'd found life as the son of one of Brazil's wealthiest businessmen to be restricting, despite all the advantages it gave him.

It couldn't have been easy, she thought, *as a young man just going out into the world, to learn that many of the people he met were more interested in his money than in him.* And if he'd had the misfortune to fall in love with women who thought of fine jewels whenever they thought of him, she could understand how he might have come to remain single for so long.

Even with her, he maintained a reserve that Melisande couldn't break through. With the exception of the few tales about his boyhood, Alex almost never spoke about himself.

Melisande had learned that his father had died when Alex was twenty-two and that his mother lived in Paris with his only sister and her French husband. He was thirty-three, had studied in the United States, and liked to sail. And that was all she knew.

He never spoke of his hopes and plans for the future, his frustrations, his friends, or his work. Though Melisande had several times talked to him at length about her work and her plans for the future, he had never reciprocated.

It was, in some ways, almost like being with a stranger. And it made her wonder just what he felt about her.

That he was physically attracted to her, Melisande did not doubt. She knew, too, that he enjoyed their rambles at least as much as she did. But beyond that . . .

Sometimes she wondered where it was all going to lead. She knew she was falling in love. Perhaps she had already. It was all so new to her she couldn't be sure.

She looked forward eagerly to their evenings out. On the nights when Alex couldn't join her and she had no other social engagement, she found it impossible to work as she'd been accustomed to doing. Whenever he wasn't there, she found herself thinking of him. He crept into her dreams, insisted on disturbing her thoughts, and disrupted the formerly orderly flow of her life.

But despite Alex's intrusion into her life, Melisande couldn't be sure just how much she had affected him. Did he think of her when she wasn't there or wish she were with him? Did he look forward to their evenings together as eagerly as she did? Or would he forget her as soon as her work in Brazil was over and she returned to the States?

Melisande had no answers, and the questions worried her. Was she wise to become so involved with a man to whom she was nothing more than a pleasant companion? And could she cope with having to leave if she *had* fallen in love—and he hadn't?

Sometimes Melisande wished she had a girlfriend with whom she could share her thoughts. She'd become very close to both Maria Sebastian and Marta Araujo, but both women had been friendly with Alex for many years. It would have been impossible to discuss such things with either of them.

And so she continued to think and to worry and to wonder.

And, every day, Carnaval drew closer.

ELEVEN

"I can't wear this! Maria, you're insane! You *know* I couldn't possibly wear anything like this!"

Melisande stared in wide-eyed shock at her image in the mirror.

"But of course you can. You look stunning. With your figure and tan, you would look great in just a tanga. With this, you look magnificent!"

Maria beamed in complacent self-satisfaction from the chair in which she had supervised her maid, who was helping Melisande into the exquisite carnaval costume.

"I swear you're trying to subvert my morals or something, Maria. First that silk dress and now this!"

Melisande gestured helplessly at the exotic creature who looked back at her from the mirror. There was nothing of the serious historian about her now. She looked, Melisande thought, like some fabulous, outrageous, and slightly risqué bird of paradise.

From the jeweled collar at her throat to the glittering, high-heeled sandals on her feet, the costume she wore sparkled with the thousands of tiny sequins and shiny beads that were sewn in a delicate, swirling pattern of blues and greens and silver on the sheer body stocking that covered her.

Covered her, Melisande amended silently, only in the sense that there was some sort of fabric against her skin. With the exception of the skimpy bikini bottom and the almost nonexistent top that did more to emphasize than to cover her high, firm breasts, the body stocking might not have existed for all that could be seen of it.

"But that's not all of the costume." Maria gestured to her maid, who picked up what appeared to be a bundle of blue and green feathers lying on a chair in the corner. "You have a crown and this tail."

As Melisande tried to twist around to see what was being attached to the back of her costume, Maria scolded, "Stand still or Rita will never get the thing on. The belt will hold it steady, and you won't have any trouble sitting down if you make sure to move the feathers out of the way first. Just like a skirt with a bustle."

"I look like a peacock," wailed Melisande as she studied the effect of the long, arching train of feathers, "and they're male!"

"Oh, Melisande, don't be ridiculous!" Maria burst into friendly laughter as she studied her friend. "You look great, and I'll feel hurt if you keep insulting the costume. I took great pains to borrow one that was very conservative, just for you."

"Conservative! What are you wearing, then? Three sequins?"

"Just about!" Maria agreed with laughing good humor. "I made Stephen's costume more restrained, of course, since he's such a stick-in-the-mud. But I don't intend to go to the Sugar Loaf

Ball looking like a dowdy frump. Carnaval is a chance to be just a little bit crazy.

"Besides," she continued more seriously, "Alex is sure to have a very fancy costume. He always does. You don't want to be a plain Jane beside him, do you? You're just as pretty, if not prettier, than any of the other women he's ever taken to a Carnaval ball, so why don't you make the most of it?"

Melisande felt a warm flush staining her cheeks at the thought of Alex's reaction to her appearance in the beautiful, exotic costume she wore. In the first shock at seeing herself in such an unaccustomed, glamorous, and, she had to admit it, sexy, costume, she hadn't thought of how others would perceive her.

Now the thought of Alex's seeing her as something other than her usual serious, conservative self was frighteningly tempting—and dangerous.

"Alex is going to be shocked. If I show up in this, looking like I-don't-know-what, he'll—" She threw up her hands in frustration. "Oh, I don't know, Maria! I just can't!"

Melisande struggled to push from her mind the tempting thought of seeing Alex's expression when he saw her costume, with her in it.

"Isn't there something else I could wear? I could have bought something in the stores if I'd known you were going to come up with this."

Maria was too intelligent and sensitive to miss the note of real fear in Melisande's voice.

"We can't change. Alex will be here in little more than half an hour, and I had a hard enough time convincing my friends to lend me this. It was lucky I had your measurements so we didn't have to go through fittings. The only costumes available this close to Carnaval are always the dumpy, ugly ones no one wants."

Her voice took on a gentle, coaxing note, as though she were talking to a recalcitrant child.

"Believe me, Alex will expect you to be in a fancy costume for the Sugar Loaf Ball. This is Brazil, not the United States. He won't think you're any less a qualified historian just because you are also a beautiful woman."

"But I've never worn anything like this in my life. This isn't me," Melisande wailed.

Maria rose from her chair and crossed the room to comfort her.

"No, it isn't you. And that's the fun of it all. Just relax and enjoy it for one evening. It's too late to back out now."

The little redhead smiled encouragingly up at Melisande. "Smile, my love. You look more like a worried chicken than a bird of paradise right now." She stepped back and gave Melisande one more approving look. "I have to get ready. Rita is going to fix your hair and do your makeup. I've told her what I want her to do, and she's very good at it. You can take off the tail feathers for now. I'll come back and check on you when I'm ready. Okay?"

Melisande nodded miserably. Even the cheerful grin Maria threw her from the door before disappearing failed to lift her gloom. With the air of one facing her doom, Melisande meekly let the maid take off the tail feathers, then seat her before the dressing-table mirror.

As she watched Rita begin to arrange her hair in a curly, feminine crown at the top of her head, Melisande struggled against the real fear welling within her.

She had always imagined that falling in love would be a heady, happy experience. Instead, she found her waking hours absorbed in an interminable struggle against thoughts of Alex, her nights full of tormenting dreams broken by long, restless hours when sleep eluded her.

Now she felt miserably frightened. Melisande had assumed, without really thinking about it, that the costume Maria would obtain for her would be something traditional—a clown, or a princess, or something that would at least cover her as much as her street clothes did.

Instead, she found herself wearing a fabulous, and very skimpy, costume that was more suited to the exotic, festive style of the beautiful Brazilian dancers who traditionally represented Carnaval in Rio.

All Melisande's carefully constructed mental defenses against her feelings were undermined by the costume. If she had been frightened by the woman she saw in Maria's elegant silk dress, she was terrified of the creature who stared, wide-eyed, from the mirror.

Now there was no tailored suit or severe bun to protect her from her own sensuality. The costume fit as though it had been sculpted to her body. Even through her fear Melisande could admit to herself that she really did look stunning. She knew Alex had said she was beautiful, but this was the first time she'd ever worn anything even remotely exotic.

Melisande was startled out of her thoughts by Rita speaking to her in soft Portuguese. The little maid was standing behind her, smiling into the mirror and holding a glittering tiara topped by smaller plumes that matched those on the cascading tail. Carefully she pinned the tiara in the curls she had arranged, then ordered Melisande to stand so she could fasten on the tail.

Frightened though she was, Melisande couldn't resist, straightening proudly to her full height as she studied the exotic creature she had become. It was a heady feeling to know that Melisande Merrick, historian, could be transformed into a dream from an *Arabian Nights'* fantasy. For a brief moment she gloried in the unaccustomed feeling of feminine beauty and power; then all her fears came rushing back.

She heard the door open behind her, and a gasp of surprise. Without turning from the mirror, she cried out, "I can't do it, Maria. I can't go out like this. This isn't me. It's too, it's too . . . too . . . What will Alex think?"

Melisande stiffened in shock as a deep voice, slightly unsteady, spoke from the doorway.

"He will think you are the most exquisite creature he has ever seen."

For a brief moment Melisande stood frozen; then she whirled, her chin held up to keep it from trembling, to see Alex crossing the room toward her. She was vaguely aware that he was dressed in a costume of gold and white that shimmered as he moved, but it was the expression in his eyes that held her attention. She didn't even notice when the maid slipped silently out of the room.

Alex's eyes were open wide, and they glittered. As he came closer she could see the pupils had expanded until his dark brown eyes looked black. His lips were parted, and his breath came audibly and unevenly from between them. His chest rose and fell rapidly in a rhythm that almost matched her own agitated breathing.

Even in high heels and drawn to her full height, Melisande had to look up at him. Her muscles trembled with tension, and sudden heat gripped her.

She started to turn away as he reached her side, but he reached out a restraining hand.

"No. Don't move. Let me look at you."

Slowly he walked around her while she fought to control her trembling.

He stood before her again, but now his eyes were warm and he smiled gently. He reached out to run a finger caressingly along her jaw.

"Why are you trembling? There's no need to be frightened. You look . . . stunning. Incredible."

Melisande wet her lips nervously.

"I'm not used to, to . . ." She waved a hand in frustration at her image in the mirror. "That's not me."

Alex's gaze met hers in the mirror. He said slowly, "Yesterday I would have agreed. But now . . ."

Though he stood beside her, he studied her image rather than turn to face her.

"Now I think I am seeing a creature I didn't even know existed. But she looks as real to me as the serious one whose glasses slide down her nose and who frowns at her notes when she's thinking, or the one who laughs with sheer pleasure when she's facing into the breeze on a sailboat."

He turned from the mirror to face her. Again, his finger caressed the line of her jaw, but this time it ran up over her chin and gently, almost imperceptibly, along her parted lips. For an interminable moment their eyes met and held; then his eyes dropped to Melisande's lips and his head bent slowly toward her.

"Haven't you gotten her to move yet, Alex? I swear I sent you in here hours ago!"

Both Melisande and Alex jerked apart, then turned toward the open door with startled haste. Alex stepped away from her, grinning ruefully.

"I was distracted, Maria. You can hardly blame me, you know."

"No, I guess I can't," Maria agreed, studying her maid's handiwork with proprietary pride. "I thought you looked great when I left you an hour ago, Melisande, but now you look stunning."

Melisande couldn't help laughing at the self-congratulatory look on Maria's face. She was grateful for the release from tension the laughter provided.

"Just what I've been telling her, but her finery seems to have her a bit worried." Alex raised a quizzical eyebrow as he smiled at Melisande.

"I *was* worried, but now that I see Maria's costume I don't feel quite so strange."

Melisande studied the brilliant, shimmering red costume of her friend. The gold and red plumes on Maria's tail spread in a magnificent arc to the ground, making Melisande's tail look sedate in comparison.

"You look wonderful. What are you, the firebird?"

"You see! I knew Melisande would appreciate my finery!" Maria clapped her hands in delight, setting her plumes quivering. "That great lout of a husband of mine just asked if I didn't think I'd be cold. In Rio! When we are going to dance all night!"

"That great lout of yours just isn't sure he wants the rest of the world to enjoy his wife's charms, too."

Stephen stood in the doorway, his slender frame clad in a tightly fitted, long-sleeved shirt and pants that were made of the same shimmering red fabric Maria had used in her own costume. The appreciative smile on his face gave the lie to his disapproving words.

"You look absolutely incredible, Melisande," he assured her with an appreciative grin. "I'm afraid you make Alex look rather drab in comparison."

"I fear you're right. And here I was wondering if all this gold wasn't just a little too much. You and I, Stephen, are going to have to spend the evening fighting off the predatory males that are going to be after our lady birds, I'm afraid."

While Maria laughingly protested against the threatened defense, Melisande studied the costume Alex wore. She was oddly comforted at finding the two conservative businessmen so at ease in their exotic finery.

Alex looked like a fantasy edition of the traditional movie pirate, with a full-sleeved shirt and pants that flared out before being tucked into tall, soft boots. The shiny gold and white fabric of the shirt and the glittery gold lamé of the pants were, however, a far cry from his usual tailored, conservative suits.

With her friends so comfortable with their fabulous costumes, Melisande let her own fears drain from her. This was Carnaval in Rio, she reminded herself. You were allowed to let your fantasies have free rein for a while.

Tonight she could play the bird of paradise to Alex's golden pirate and the world would not spin from its place. Tomorrow, she thought, she could put her hair into a tight little bun at the nape of her neck, don her glasses and a comfortable skirt and blouse, and sit down to her work as she always had.

But tonight she was free. She laughed out loud and her eyes sparkled. Tonight she would not be afraid of anything—not of herself or of Alex or of anything.

With the full tails of Maria's and Melisande's costumes filling all the available space, even Alex's big limousine seemed small. The chauffeur had to help them untangle all the feathers before they could get out. They stood on the pavement of the parking lot, laughing in excitement at the colorful crowd that swirled around them.

When they joined the line of partygoers waiting for the next cable car to take them to the top of Sugar Loaf, the last of Melisande's fears disappeared completely. Maria had been right—her costume *was* conservative. Some of the older couples were clad in traditional full costumes, but the young men and women clustering about and laughing were more notable for what they weren't wearing than for what they were. Some women wore little more than a few strings and net hose, all topped off by fantastic plumes and imaginative creations of net and sequins.

Melisande caught sight of a rainbow-hued butterfly, complete with spreading wings, and a golden dragon with ruby eyes. A brilliantly colored peacock bowed and scraped before her, chattering in Portuguese, before Alex drove him off with a laugh. An elegant swan in delicate white feathers reclaimed him.

"He thought your blue and green would go better with his costume and offered me his swan, since her white would match my gold and white."

Alex helped her onto the waiting cable car, his face alight with a boyish enthusiasm Melisande had never seen before.

"What did you tell him?"

"That while most pirates have a pet parrot, I have a bird of paradise and am not about to let her go."

Melisande found herself pushed against Alex's broad chest as one more couple crowded onto the cable car before the doors were shut and they started off. Though the car was carrying less than half of its usual complement of passengers, many of the costumes took up the space of two or three people.

From over Alex's protective arm Melisande could see Stephen and Maria talking animatedly to a couple dressed all in silver. She waved as she caught Maria's eye, then jumped in surprise as a hand brushed along her thigh.

"Sorry." Alex's mouth was close to her ear to enable her to hear him above the din in the crowded car. "I was trying to get your tail out of the way of that Indian mogul over there. We'll have more room once we reach the top."

The cable car rose first to the hill below Sugar

Loaf, Urca Mountain, then rapidly glided up the dark mass of Sugar Loaf looming above them. Melisande caught her breath at the splendor visible from the car window. Rio sparkled below them, the tall buildings and wide boulevards arcing in a brilliant crescent against the black outline of Copacabana beach.

"It's beautiful," she said softly, then looked up quickly as Alex bent low above her, trying to catch her words through the noise. "It's beautiful!" she shouted, and grinned with excitement.

"We'll be at the top in a minute. You can hear the samba band now."

Vaguely Melisande could make out the primitive, imperative thump of the samba drums, their irresistible beat growing ever stronger as the cable car swept smoothly up. By the time the car stopped at the terminal the beat was so strong it surged over even the excited chatter of the passengers rushing out to join the colorful crowd thronging the lighted area on top.

Melisande started to follow the crowd out of the car, but stopped and looked over her shoulder in surprise as Alex knelt to straighten the plumes of her tail.

"My bird of paradise has to have all her feathers in order before she goes out in public."

He grinned up at her as he gave a last shake to the plumes, then slowly straightened. He was so close she could feel the heat of him, the lean, masculine power of him, yet he never touched her.

Melisande grinned in return and gave a little wiggle that set her tail to quivering enticingly. She laughed in excitement and sprang from the car onto the platform, then grabbed Alex's hand as he appeared beside her.

"Come on! There are Stephen and Maria!"

The four of them plunged into the excited mass of laughing, shouting dancers moving to the incessant beating of the samba drums.

The night, hot and humid, surrounded them. The brilliant lights strung about them created a world that had no contact with the normal life of the city glittering below.

As they mixed in the crowd, Alex, Maria, and Stephen discovered friends behind the fanciful costumes. Their group grew, then shrank as people joined them, then faded back into the press of people. Melisande danced with Alex, with Stephen, and with a spaceman decked out in a rainbow of flashing lights and little else.

"I thought only the women wore skimpy costumes," she gasped as the spaceman returned her to Alex, who offered her a refreshing sip of the drink he held.

"Not necessarily," he said, grinning. "Almost anything goes during Carnaval. And with the attention you're drawing, I'd better dance with you now before I lose you to the African warrior who's been asking about you."

With a laugh, Melisande was swept back into the crowd.

TWELVE

The wild dance was enough to set a dead man's heart to racing. Alex was far from dead, but it wasn't the dance or the music that stirred him so. All around him people writhed and stomped and laughed in a samba frenzy, yet they might have been on the other side of the moon for all the attention he paid them.

His attention was focused on the brilliant blue-green fantasy spinning in front of him, eyes alight with the sheer joy of the music and the moment. The beat of the samba drums was an irresistible enticement, and Melisande's slender, supple body moved with an unconsciously arousing grace that stirred wild thoughts of flinging her over his shoulder and fleeing into the night like a pirate with his booty.

Too bad the short sword at his side was nothing but gilt. He'd happily have hacked his way through the crowd if it meant he could have her all to himself, with only the night to hold them.

How many Carnavals had he been to? Alex wondered. The first one he remembered, he'd been three. There must have been one or two somewhere along the way that he'd had to miss because of school or work or travel, but there hadn't been many. Say, twenty-five to make a nice, round number?

Twenty-five Carnavals, yet he felt as if he were seeing one for the first time.

In a way, he was, because he was seeing it through Melisande's eyes, savoring with her the excitement and the heady air of abandon, relishing the un-abashed sensuality of it just as she relished it. What-ever doubts she'd had while standing in front of Maria's mirror had vanished in the colorfully garbed crowd that surrounded them. Once she'd mingled with the celebrants on Sugar Loaf, she'd relaxed and thrown herself into a wholehearted enjoyment of the ball.

Unfortunately, Alex wasn't the only man in the crowd who was enjoying her beauty and grace and her obvious delight in the moment. Another dancer—an absurdly handsome, well-built, half-na-ked man—suddenly appeared to claim her hand.

Melisande laughed and shook her head so that her plumes trembled, but the stranger was not to be denied. As Alex watched her swing away on the arm of another man—you were not allowed to cling to your original partner at a Carnaval ball, no mat-ter how much you wanted to—he wasn't at all sure he approved of the heady exuberance he'd always taken for granted. Not if it meant he had to give up his bird of paradise to another man.

"What a forlorn-looking pirate you are, my friend!" Maria appeared at his side as suddenly as if she'd materialized out of thin air. Her face was aglow with the excitement of the partying she loved. "Don't tell me Melisande has deserted you for an-other!"

He nodded wryly. "Stolen from me by an Adonis in a loincloth so small that even Tarzan would blush."

"Poor Alex!" Her grin of delight carried not a trace of sympathy.

"It's all your fault, you know. If you hadn't invited us—"

"Then you wouldn't have seen Melisande in that incredible costume, and she wouldn't have had a chance to enjoy one of the delights of Rio." She thumped his arm in mock anger with her small fist. "And don't tell me you're sorry because I won't believe a word of it."

"Not sorry—"

Maria laughed knowingly. "Jealous, more like. I know the signs."

"You ought to. You led Stephen a merry dance, once upon a time. I felt sorry for the poor guy, but he was too besotted to listen." The words were for Maria, but his gaze was fixed on Melisande, who was half-buried in the crowd.

But not so buried that he missed the flashing smile she bestowed on her kidnapper, who was leaning close to catch what she was saying. Too close, damn it!

Without his willing it, Alex's hands curved into fists and his teeth clamped shut so hard a muscle twinged in his jaw.

Maria didn't miss any of it. "You *are* jealous!" she crowed, delighted. "I knew it!"

Alex jumped. "Me? Ridiculous!" He waved a hand to indicate just how ridiculous the notion was. ' I'm never jealous. You know that."

"I know, but you are now!" She gave a triumphant laugh. "It's about time you got your come-uppance, Alex Robeson," she added, poking him in the chest with the tip of one scarlet-painted finger, "and I have a feeling our Dr. Merrick is just the woman to give it to you."

"And you call yourself a friend!" he said, feigning horror.

Suddenly, there wasn't a hint of amusement in her expression. "I *am* your friend," she said firmly, "but you're long overdue for a fall."

"Me? For what?"

She cocked her head, studying him. "For taking most women for granted. For not trusting them."

He frowned down at her. "Just what do you think it is Melisande is going to do to me that no other woman has ever done?"

Her eyes narrowed until the glitter she'd scattered so generously across her lids seemed like dragons' eyes glaring at him. "I don't know . . . yet."

He snorted, uncertain whether he ought be amused, or irritated. "Well, I don't know either, so don't try to bully me, Maria Sebastian. It didn't work when we were kids, and it's not going to work now."

She tossed her head in haughty dismissal. "Hah!"

That enchanting grin of hers was back with a vengeance. It made him a little nervous, wondering what the grin portended.

All she said was, "We'll see. But in the meantime, I think I'll let you dance with me, whether you deserve the privilege or not."

"And if I don't?"

She laughed. "You don't have a choice in the matter," she said, and, without giving him a chance to protest, she dragged him off, back into the whirling, stomping crowd.

The night, the music, and the constant stream of compliments that flowed her way were a heady mix for Melisande. They had come late to the ball in order to give it time to get into full swing, and it *was* swinging. She didn't even care that the term was horribly out of date because it was the only one that could describe the madness.

Energy raced through her so, she scarcely paused in the heady whirl of dancing and laughter. She'd met some of the dancers at other parties, and the wild, gay informality of the ball made it possible to dance with others she didn't know and never saw again after they disappeared into the crush of people surrounding her.

But always she found her way back to Alex, or he found her. There was a magnetism between them that drew them together no matter how much the dancing had separated them.

And when they met, sparks flew.

"What? Not tired yet?" he demanded, laughing, after the peacock who had tried to trade her for a swan had finally managed to claim her for a dance. "I've lost track of the men who've stolen you from me."

"Don't even try to count that high!" she boldly shot back. "And it's just as well. I don't want to know how many gorgeous women have dragged *you* away, either."

"But only after you'd already abandoned me," he said, leaning close. There was laughter in his eyes

and on his lips, but she sensed something else in
him, as well. Something possessive and almost . . .
feral beneath his apparently careless teasing.

She shook her head, startled by the absurd fancy.
When she looked into his eyes again, whatever it
was she'd thought she'd seen was gone. If it had
ever been there in the first place, she reminded herself. Chances were, the night air and the excitement
of the ball had affected her overheated brain.

"I'm not abandoning you now," he said, and,
wrapping his arm around her waist, drew her back
into the dance.

The difference was, this time he didn't let her go.
He held her so tightly that she couldn't help pressing against him—breast, belly, hip, thigh. They
might have been welded together. If so, the fire
from the welding was still there, flaming where they
joined, burning her skin.

"You can't dance the samba like this!" she protested. It was hard to get the words out, hard to
breathe.

"*I* can." He gave her a pirate grin and swung her
about in a move that sucked the last molecule of
air from her lungs.

It wasn't the samba. It was something wilder,
fiercer—something even more primitively erotic.
Anyplace else, dancing like this would have been a
clumsy effort, her every movement hampered by
her own uncertainties and embarrassment as much
as by his intimate hold on her. But not now. Social
restraints were loosened, and her blood was running hot and sweet and hungry. Somehow, despite
the crowd, she found herself moving with him as if

her body were a part of his and his were a part of hers.

Molten heat rushed through her, coupled with a desire so sharp and aching that it pierced her like a sword. Just as she thought she might spontaneously burst into flame, the drums thundered to a halt, leaving her ears ringing and her head spinning.

"*Now* what do you say?" Alex demanded, leaning close so that his lips brushed the shell of her ear. "Still think I can't dance the samba with you in my arms? Hmmm?"

His hand slid up her spine, holding her as he bent her backward, forcing her body to arch into his even more intimately than before.

Melisande gasped and clasped her hands around his neck. She couldn't have stopped herself from bending to his demanding touch if she'd wanted to . . . and she didn't.

It didn't matter that the drums had stopped, either, for her heart was pounding hard and fast enough to take their place. Her chest rose and fell as she struggled to regain her breath. The motion made her achingly aware of his own rapid breathing and of how broad and hard his chest was.

"Unhand that woman, fiend!" Stephen Sebastian cried, suddenly emerging from the crowd. Maria was glued to his side, her face flushed, eyes sparkling.

With a laugh, Alex swept Melisande back upright, only to pull her tight against his side so that she could hear his heart pounding with a wild beat to match her own. "You can't have my woman, Sebastian."

Stephen grinned. "Do you really think I'd try for her with *this* firebird on my arm?"

"Hah!" said Maria with a challenging grin. She turned to Melisande. "Some friends have grabbed a spot with a great view of the city. We're headed that way and thought you two might like to join us for a drink and a bite to eat."

Was she glad of the interruption? Melisande wondered as she and Alex followed the Sebastians through the crowd. What might have happened if Stephen and Maria hadn't appeared to break the spell that had held her in its grip?

The questions got lost in the confusion of meeting the Sebastians' friends, then finding something to eat and drink. Though Alex stayed by her side through most of it, the press of people and the noise of lively conversations on all sides made thought impossible.

She didn't have a chance to find out afterward, either, for one of Stephen's friends, over Alex's laughing protests, claimed her for a dance, then another swept her away until Melisande found herself separated from Alex once again. Frequently, she caught glimpses of him in the crowd—always with a beautiful woman as his partner—but the mad circle of the dance never brought them back together.

When she at last dropped, panting, from the crowd of dancers, she looked for his dark head among the tossing plumes and feathers but couldn't see him. Stifling a twinge of disappointment, she pushed her way through the crowd, headed for one of the tables where she could claim a drink of cold water. Suddenly an arm swept around her and she was pulled from her feet and against a broad chest clad in gold and white.

"My bird of paradise has decided to come back to the roost for a little while?"

"For a while," she said, laughing and throwing her arms around his neck.

Alex's flashing dark eyes met hers. It might have been her imagination, or a lingering madness from the dance, but she thought she could read a promise in those depths, and a question. A dangerous question that made her heart skip a beat and her stomach tighten—whether in fear or excitement, she couldn't have said.

The sequins and beads on her body stocking pressed into her skin, yet she could feel the hard muscles of his chest and stomach and thighs as clearly as though nothing were separating them. The heat that washed through her at the feel of him had nothing to do with the warm night that wrapped around them.

"Then let's find a perch from which you can't escape too easily." Alex set her on her feet, but kept his arm protectively around her waist as he pushed a way for them through the crowd.

A waiter passed with a tray loaded with icy drinks, and Alex stopped him to claim two frosty glasses.

"Over here. The view can't be beat, and we can find a rock to sit on."

There was no way to escape from the mass of partyers thronging the top of Sugar Loaf, but Alex did find them an unoccupied corner where the sound of the band was slightly muted and where they ran no risk of being trampled by the dancers.

"We'll put the drinks down here for the moment," he said, taking the glass from Melisande's hand, "then we'll put you up here."

Before Melisande realized what he was about, his hands came around her waist and he tossed her up to a perch on an outcrop of rock.

Melisande found herself gazing down into his upturned face, both of her hands on his shoulders where she had put them for support as he'd picked her up. Her breath caught in her throat at the hunger that burned in his gaze, but before she could react he stepped back, hands on hips, to inspect her with a proprietorial air.

"Watch your tail. You're sitting on it."

"No, I'm not, it just looks that way because it's so big. Come on up," said Melisande, patting the rock beside her.

"I'm rather admiring the view from down here. I like the way the lights flash from all those sequins, but I like the bare skin I can see underneath even better."

"Then come and admire it from up close," said Melisande with a seductive insouciance she hadn't known she possessed. "I'll even move my tail."

Before she could rearrange any of the plumes that spread about her Alex had bounded up beside her. His hand grazed her thigh as he brushed aside the mass of blue and green, leaving a burning trail on her skin under the sheer fabric of her costume.

He leaned toward her, and again her breath caught as her eyes met his.

"You're right. The view is better from up here."

He leaned closer still, and Melisande felt her heart begin to pound, matching the hypnotic, sensual beat of the samba drums in the background.

Her lips parted, quivered. The sequins on her breast flashed as her chest rose and fell with her suddenly quickened breathing.

"Melisande." Her name came in a trembling whisper. His hand lifted to caress her face. His fingers burned her skin as they gently ran along the side of her cheek and down her throat, lingering where her pulse throbbed above the jeweled collar she wore.

His fingers slid behind her neck and his thumb gently forced her chin up. Slowly, achingly slowly, his head came down to meet hers. Their lips met, gently at first. Melisande heard a gasp, but didn't know if it had escaped his trembling lips, or hers.

Alex's head came up slightly, and his eyes burned into hers. "Oh, God, Melisande, you're so deliciously sweet."

He groaned and brought his lips down to meet hers with a driving, hungry force that obliterated the world around them.

Dawn was tentatively touching the buildings of Ipanema when the limousine drew up at the door. They'd dropped off Stephen and Maria at their apartment first, and Melisande had promised to drop by later in the day to pick up the clothes she'd left there.

Now, as Alex handed her out of the car, she looked up at the golden light staining the building. She was tired, but the excitement of the night still stirred within her.

Alex finished giving his directions to the chauffeur and came to stand beside her on the pavement, watching the spreading light.

"I feel a little like Cinderella," Melisande confessed as she turned to him. "Only I made it past midnight. For me, it's the morning light that transforms the magic."

Alex's arm went around her waist as he gazed down at her. "Why does the magic have to end? Is the light of day so harsh?"

"Not end." Melisande reached out to touch his cheek gently. "Transform."

He turned beneath her touch to press a gentle kiss to her fingertips. "Do you believe in fairy tales?"

"I never did before."

"And now?"

With his arm around her, Melisande thought, she could believe in anything he wanted her to believe in. But she couldn't say that. The light of day brought an unwelcome touch of reality with it, yet there was always the possibility that reality itself had changed because of the night's magic.

"Now?" It came out as scarcely more than a whisper, a fleeting breath of doubt. She shook her head, uncertain. Her crown of plumes waved gently, unaffected by the long night of dancing.

Still within the circle of his arms, she shifted to watch as the morning light spread across the front of the building, turning the broad panes of glass to molten gold.

Alex bent closer. "*Do* you believe in fairy tales, Melisande?" he asked again, softly. His eyes glowed with a fire to equal the morning's dawning light.

"I don't know." A swift smile crossed her lips.

"I'll have to check with my fairy godmother and get back to you."

His answering laugh warmed her. "All right, I'll accept that. But don't take too long, will you?"

Alex rode up with her in the elevator, then took her apartment key and inserted it in the lock. He started to turn the key, but stopped and turned to her instead. Melisande sensed within him the same change in mood that suddenly washed through her: once the door was opened reality would return and they would leave behind them the excitement, the magic, that had been theirs for a few brief hours.

Had those hours wrought any changes in their comfortable reality? Melisande wondered. She pushed away the thought, knowing that she wasn't at all sure what she wanted the answer to be.

He leaned closer. "I think I'll say good-bye to my bird of paradise out here, before Melisande Merrick, historian, returns." His voice was soft, caressing.

Only their lips touched in a gentle, lingering kiss, yet Melisande felt the same warmth, less urgent but no less sweet, that had thrilled through her when he had held her in his arms on Sugar Loaf and kissed her with a demanding hunger that gave no quarter.

His head lifted slightly from hers, and his eyes roamed her face as though seeking an answer to a question Melisande could not fathom. His pupils had expanded until only a narrow rim of dark brown iris remained to be seen. It was, Melisande thought, like looking into a bottomless well. Then his lips quirked in a gentle, ironic smile, and he straightened.

"Sweet dreams, Melisande," he said.

And he stepped into the waiting elevator and was gone.

THIRTEEN

The elevator was attractively paneled in wood, polished to a smooth finish, and dimly lit, but Alex didn't see any of it. His mind's eye was fixed on images that were as far away as Sugar Loaf and as close as the apartment just a few floors above his head. The opening elevator doors made him start in surprise.

Like a dreamer emerging from a dream, he blinked, straightened, then slowly walked out of the elevator, across the lobby, and onto the street. His chauffeur was lounging by the limo, but snapped to attention and swung the car door open as Alex emerged from the building.

Alex eyed the open door with disfavor. He'd planned to go directly home, get some sleep, then spend the afternoon in his office. Suddenly none of that held any appeal.

He studied the street around him, uncertain what to do next but quite sure that he did not want to go home, and that he wouldn't sleep if he did. Not yet.

"Wait here for me, will you, João?" he told his driver. "I'm going for a walk."

The man nodded, unfazed. His bland gaze slid

over Alex's costume. "Would you care to leave your . . . um . . . your sword, sir?"

"My— Oh!" Alex grimaced as he glanced down at his clothes, then shrugged. He wouldn't be the first to greet a new day still dressed in his Carnaval costume, and he was quite sure he wouldn't be the last, but the gilt sword was carrying things just a little too far.

"Here. And get yourself some breakfast, while you're at it, why don't you," he added, handing the man some money along with the sword. "Don't rush."

João grinned. "She *is* very beautiful, sir," he said, cheerfully pocketing the cash.

Alex grinned back. "She is, indeed."

Despite the early hour, the streets were already filling with people on their way to work or church or a local café for a morning cup of coffee, which would be taken at leisure along with a sweet, fresh pastry and a morning paper. Neither the pastry nor the paper held much appeal, but Alex had to admit that the thought of coffee was appealing.

A small café across the street beckoned. Alex lined up at the counter for a quick espresso. He was the only one still clad in party garb, but other than a quick, smiling glance or a knowing wink, no one seemed to pay much attention to him. This was Rio, after all, and Carnaval. A man was entitled to enjoy the celebration, and it wouldn't have been a good party if it had shut down before dawn.

A young, dark-haired woman drifted in, yawning mightily, and took a seat at a table by the window. She was clad in jeans and a T-shirt, but her tumbled hair still showed traces of the previous night's elaborate hairdo. Though she'd obviously washed off most of her makeup, traces of glitter still sparkled on her eyelids and cheeks. The sight reminded Alex of the glitter that had colored Melisande's eyelids and the sequins that had dotted her costume.

He wrenched his gaze away and tried to concentrate on the pattern of the floor tile instead. Frowning, he poked at a dried coffee stain with the toe of his shoe.

Maybe he should have asked Melisande out for coffee. If he'd given her a chance to change into something mundane like jeans and a T-shirt, maybe he would have been able to forget the unsettling memories of her in that fantasic costume, of her caught in the frenzy of the dance, of her body pressing against his, thigh against thigh, hip against hip—

The customer behind him in line nudged him slightly.

Alex brought his head up with a snap. "What—?"

"Do you want to order?" the man inquired irritably. He nodded at the young man behind the counter. "He's asked you twice already."

"Oh. Sorry." Alex moved up to the counter. "Double espresso. Extra sugar."

The clerk grinned. "Good party, huh?"

"Uh . . . yeah." Alex swore silently. He could feel the heat rising at the back of his neck, and this time it had nothing to do with the memory of Melisande or the hours just past.

"She must be pretty special."

"What?"

"The girl." The clerk gave three quick jerks on the lever of the coffee grinder, then thunked the freshly filled coffee holder into its slot on the espresso machine. "You don't look like the kind of guy who would be worn out by one Carnaval party, so it must have been the girl."

It was.

Alex didn't say it. He grunted instead and dug into his pocket for some change.

"Next time," the clerk said, still grinning, "you bring her here for coffee afterward. If she looks as good the morning after as she looked the night before, you'll know for sure that she's the one."

Alex blinked and dropped a coin, then dropped another coin as he bent to retrieve the first.

He didn't bother to count the change, just slapped the whole handful on the counter. There was more than enough there for two double espressos and a good tip, besides.

"Double espresso, extra sugar," the clerk said, sliding the filled paper cup across the counter. He swept up the coins in one smooth, practiced motion.

"Thanks." Alex took a quick sip of the hot, flavorful brew, and sighed.

The clerk's grin widened. "You need more, you let me know."

"I just might do that," Alex said as he turned and headed toward the door.

"And don't forget what I said," the clerk called out, loud enough for everyone to hear. "You know, about the way she looks the morning after!"

It was early afternoon when Melisande finally awoke. She stretched luxuriously, aware of a sense of well-being that had nothing to do with her stiff, aching muscles.

She picked up her robe from the bedside chair, slipped it on, then padded down the hall to the kitchen to beg a cup of coffee and a sandwich from a delighted and indulgent Senhora Amado.

A long soak in a hot bath, followed by an invigorating cold shower, served to dispel some of her aches and restore Melisande to her usual lively self. When she called Maria she found her friend had just woken up, but would be delighted to have her come for her clothes and stay for a late lunch. Knowing that she wouldn't be able to do any work in the hours that remained of the day, Melisande accepted the invitation with pleasure.

Anxious to work out the last of the soreness in her muscles, Melisande decided to walk to her friends' apartment. The familiar, crowded streets seemed different today, somehow brighter and more alive than before. She walked down them as though in a pleasant dream, her thoughts far away. When she discovered that, by standing still and closing her eyes, she could almost feel Alex's lips on her, she stopped often.

Melisande found her irrepressible red-haired friend bursting to discuss the ball and delighted by some photos that had just been delivered by a professional photographer who had taken pictures of the dancers the night before.

"Look, Melisande. They're really good. Stephen said I was crazy to agree to buy some of the pictures, but they've turned out wonderfully and the guy who took them delivered them right away, just like he promised."

Maria bounced on the sofa in her eagerness to show the pictures to Melisande.

"I'm going to frame this one of Stephen and me. He's usually so serious when he gets his picture taken. I like the way his smile came out."

"You're right," Melisande agreed. "You two look great."

"And this one is even better. It's of you and Alex. This copy is for you; I've already ordered another one for Alex."

Melisande took the picture Maria held out to her, then gasped in delighted surprise. The photographer had taken the picture with the black rock behind them, rather than the usual crowd of other dancers. He had caught them in a moment when Alex had his arm around her waist and was looking down at the exotic creature beside him and laughing. And she herself, Melisande had to admit, looked stunning. Her costume blazed with reflected light, and she had been standing in a way that made the most of her slender figure. Her head was raised proudly, gracefully, as she looked up to the tall man beside her and shared in his joyous laughter.

"Why, it's a wonderful picture, Maria. Thank you very much."

Though she knew it was foolish to let her fantasies have their way with her, the picture seemed like a tangible promise for the future, proof that there was something more ahead for them, something sweeter, richer, wilder.

Melisande carefully put it beside her purse, wondering what Alex would think of it when he got his copy.

The two women shared a light meal while they

continued to discuss the ball, laughing over the escapades of some of the dancers, commenting on the sometimes incredible costumes that had been worn.

When Melisande at last rose to take her leave Maria said, "I've talked Stephen into taking the actual day of Carnaval, this Tuesday, off so we can go sailing again. That's why he went in to the office today—he said he'd need a clear conscience for Tuesday. The city will be crazy, doing up Carnaval with a bang before Ash Wednesday and the start of Lent. We can go down the coast, have lunch like we did before. Stephen is going to invite Alex, too. Will you come?"

The idea had been tempting, even before Maria had mentioned Alex, and Melisande accepted the invitation with pleasure. Walking home, she found herself humming happily and swinging her clothes bag like a schoolgirl.

She shouldn't read too much into last night, she reminded herself. Or into the kiss this morning.

But how could she help it? How did you tell your heart to stop beating or your head to stop dreaming? Why would you want to?

After all, she wasn't some foolish teenager. She'd had enough men in her life to know she wasn't swayed by a handsome face or a smooth line of talk, and she wasn't about to lose her emotional footing now. But that didn't mean she wasn't going to enjoy the pleasures of the moment. She wouldn't let Alex hurt her. He wouldn't try.

Melisande arrived back at the apartment just as the phone was ringing. The deep, masculine voice on the other end of the line brought a delighted smile to her face.

"You survived, then," he said. "I don't know about you, but I'm still stiff from all that dancing."

His rich baritone stirred her as though he were standing there beside her.

"Too much paper-pushing," she teased. "You should adopt a more active lifestyle, like me."

"Active lifestyle? What would a historian know about that?"

"Try lugging around some of those old books sometime. You'd find out quickly enough."

His laughter was like whipped cream and chocolate, rich and infinitely tempting.

"All right," he said. "I'll admit you held up pretty well at the ball. I'm surprised you even survived, as often as you were out there dancing. I swear you put us all to shame."

She laughed. There was a long pause.

"I wanted to thank you," he said at last, softly. "For last night. For"—he stopped, seemed to consider his words—"well, for sharing your pleasure in the experience. I guess I've been to so many Carnaval balls, I'd forgotten just how much fun they can be. So . . . thank you."

"Thank *you.*" Melisande kept her voice low and controlled, but she couldn't control the happiness that sang through her. There seemed to be a world of promises in those few simple words of his.

No, that wasn't right. The promise lay in the way he said them, in the warmth she heard, and in the way his voice dipped, ever so slightly, there at the end.

Her mother had been right all along: it's not what you say, but how you say it that counts.

Or how you don't say anything at all, she amended
silently, listening to the soft sound of Alex's breathing at the other end of the phone, remembering.

"Would you join me for dinner tonight?" he
asked, breaking into her dangerous reverie. "I know
of a wonderful restaurant on the coast south of
Ipanema. The food and wine are superb and you
can hear the sea wash up on the rocks below. It's
a . . . magical place. I think you'd like it."

There was a brief pause. Melisande had to struggle to keep from laughing out loud from delight.

"Will you come?"

"Yes, thank you," she said. "I'd love to."

"Good."

Melisande didn't miss the note of satisfaction in
his voice. What felt like an electric charge tingled
up her arm, then down her spine, setting her nerves
alight.

"I'll come by for you at seven-thirty, then. And,
Melisande?"

She didn't miss the hesitancy as he spoke her
name, either.

"Yes, Alex?"

"Take care," he said softly, and hung up.

Melisande stood before the open closet contemplating the neatly hung clothes. The white silk, she
knew, would be the most appropriate while still being properly conservative. But she found herself
reaching instead for the elegant green silk from Maria Sebastian's shop.

She hesitated, frowning, then slid it farther along
the rack and took down the simple white sheath she

had worn to Marta's cocktail party, her first social event in Brazil. Laying it across the bed she quickly and skillfully put on her makeup in a way that highlighted her natural, delicate coloring and accented the green of her eyes. A touch of perfume, and then she pulled on the white dress and started to brush her hair back into its usual bun.

But one heavy strand slipped from her hand to fall in a shiny mass of waves to her shoulder. She reached for it, then paused and frowned at her neat image in the mirror. With an abrupt tug, Melisande loosened her hair completely. She hesitated again, biting her lower lip, before unzipping the white dress and flinging it on the bed.

She stepped to the closet and pulled out the green silk dress, studied its graceful, shimmering folds. Even though she'd paid Maria for the gown, much against her friend's wishes, she'd never worn it since that day when she'd tried it on in the shop.

Then she had been shocked and frightened by the sensuous, sexy woman who had looked out at her from the mirror. But after having found the courage to wear the exotic Carnaval costume Maria had found for her, it didn't seem so terrifying to show the world the Melisande Merrick who had been hidden for so long.

She thought of how Alex would look when he saw her in it, and that was enough.

And don't forget what I said, the clerk had called after him as he'd left that little café that morning. *You know, about the way she looks the morning after.*

And what about the way she looks the evening after?

Alex wondered as he deftly slid his Mercedes sports car into the cramped parking place not far from Melisande's apartment building.

He shut off the engine and pulled the key out of the ignition, but made no move to get out of the car.

That morning, he'd spent the good part of an hour wandering the streets of Ipanema. He hadn't gone near the beach; he had a disconcerting feeling that it would remind him too much of how she'd looked that first morning he'd met her, glorious in a body-hugging green swimsuit that somehow contrived to look incredibly sexy on her despite its conservative cut.

Instead, he'd wandered through the tree-shaded, crowded streets, sipping his first espresso, then a second that he bought at a different cafe—one where the clerk, a stolid old man with a sagging face and receding hairline, was more interested in returning to the tall stool he kept behind the counter than in prying into his customers' love lives.

As he'd walked, Alex had found himself thinking of Melisande, of the way she looked, of all the different faces she'd presented to him in the relatively short time he'd known her.

He thought of her now as he gazed up at her apartment building, remembering the vague, soft-eyed, myopic stare of that first meeting; the sparkling look of excitement with which she greeted every new experience, every new sight; the intense expression of concentration that meant she was engrossed in her research and had forgotten the rest of the world existed.

He couldn't remember ever being so acutely aware of a woman, even when she wasn't with him. *Especially* when she wasn't with him.

It was disconcerting. It wasn't at all what he was accustomed to.

It was . . . dangerous.

The word shocked him. Melisande? *Dangerous?* He'd known unweaned kittens that were tougher than she was.

And yet . . .

With a soft oath, Alex slid out of the car and slammed the door behind him, then crossed the street to Melisande's apartment building . . . and to Melisande.

FOURTEEN

The dress flowed over her shoulders and settled about her with a soft rustle. Against her skin the fabric was cool, sensual, enticing. With every movement the colors shifted in the light, from green to blue to blue-green to silver and back again, highlighting her slender figure and creamy skin.

As she stared at her image in the mirror Melisande felt the fear of that hidden Melisande rising within her. The woman she'd kept inside her for so long was more sensual, more daring, more . . . *alive*.

She might as well have spoken the word aloud. It seemed to vibrate in the air around her, an almost audible reminder that there was, that there ought to be, something beyond the shadowed confines of the archives and libraries and museums where she passed so much of her professional life.

Alive. Melisande glanced at the wide-eyed, vibrant woman in the mirror. Her chin came up a fraction of an inch; her back straightened. *Alive*.

Before she could change her mind again she picked up her silver evening clutch and left the room, walking softly along the thickly carpeted hallway and into the living room.

She was halfway into the big room before she noticed that the sliding glass doors to the balcony were open. The soft lighting of the room and the darkness behind the doors combined to turn the glass into mirrors which reflected her graceful figure, obscuring the balcony behind. She reached out to close the first door when, with a start, she realized that she was not alone.

"Good evening, Melisande," came a soft voice as Alex stepped from the dark balcony into the lighted room.

Her eyes widened in surprise as she glanced up into his face, suddenly confused by his nearness. It had been so much easier when the samba drums had filled the air with their insistent rhythms and she and Alex had been surrounded by laughing, excited people happily wrapped in the moment's fantasy.

"What, cat got your tongue?" He stepped nearer, then suddenly bent and kissed her, lightly, on the lips.

"A quick kiss to awaken a sleeping beauty," he said softly. "I watched you walking through that lighted room to my dark balcony, and I thought how like a sleeping beauty you seemed. Not at all my exotic bird of paradise."

"The colors are the same."

"Yes, silver and green and blue. This dress is like you, Melisande."

His voice was unexpectedly husky. With one long finger he traced a fold of fabric that fell from her shoulder and across her breast to gather at her slender waist.

How was it, Melisande wondered, fighting the fire that suddenly rose within her, that he could affect her so easily? His finger hadn't even touched *her,* merely slid along the edge of the delicate silk, yet she could feel her body responding in spite of herself.

"The dress is like me?" she said faintly, shaken by the contact that wasn't really any contact at all.

He nodded, his eyes alight with an inner fire. "Exactly like you," he said. "Delicate. Beautiful. Never the same from one moment to the next, but always beautiful. Always."

"Always?" She could only whisper.

"Always," he whispered before his lips met hers and he could say no more.

The fire within her raged higher, responding to the fire Melisande could feel burning in the lips that moved so ruthlessly, so demandingly against hers. Her arms slid around him as he pulled her more tightly against him.

"Alex," she whimpered, clinging to him as his lips left hers to trace a trail of fire along the line of her jaw and down her throat to the heated skin of her bare shoulder. "Alex."

Her only answer was a groan as Alex's fingers tangled in her hair, forcing her head down against the fine cloth of his suit. She could hear his heart pounding in his chest and feel his labored breathing.

"This is crazy." His voice trembled like the fingers that were trying to smooth her tumbled hair.

"I know."

Melisande's response was muffled because her head was still pressed against his chest, her body burrowed in the safety of the strong arm that held her so tightly.

I love you, she thought, *I love you. It's crazy, and I still love you.*

She closed her eyes and struggled to push all thought from her mind. With his arms around her, she felt safe and wanted, and for right now, for this moment, it was enough.

"You'd better comb your hair." His laugh was shaky, but surer than his voice had been a moment before.

Gently he put her from him and stepped back, his eyes dark wells, his breathing still uneven. "Our reservations are for eight, and it doesn't do to keep Lourdes waiting."

"Lourdes?"

Melisande was vaguely pleased at the calmness with which she could speak, though she could feel the blood still pounding in her throat.

"You'll see. If I don't get distracted again."

Going down in the elevator Melisande strove to keep the conversation light, and was glad to see that Alex was just as anxious as she to keep the evening on a safer basis than it had started.

"What!" she exclaimed in mock indignation when he guided her across the street to the Mercedes. "No limousine?"

He grinned as he helped her in. "I would have brought the Ferrari, but it's rather hard to climb into."

They were soon purring up the winding coast road which began at the south end of Ipanema beach. Dark hillside loomed to their right, while the cliffside houses to their left interrupted at intervals their view of a sea glowing with reflected moonlight.

Neither spoke. To Melisande, wrapped in the comforting darkness, the silence was too intensely intimate for conversation. She was acutely aware of Alex beside her, and from his glances over at her, she knew he was just as aware of her.

"I hope the dinner tonight will be a pleasant one," he said at last, slowing the Mercedes and turning into a drive illuminated by lights placed along a tall wall and among the heavy vines and flowering plants of a garden parking area.

He parked and came to open her door, taking her arm to help her. Melisande moved quickly, disturbed by her sudden response to his touch, and stumbled slightly.

His grip tightened as his other hand reached around to support her. She could feel his breath in her hair and the warmth of his powerful body so close to hers.

"Are you all right? This gravel can be tricky in your high heels."

She nodded dumbly, unable to speak, overwhelmed by the rushing heat he could ignite so easily.

Then, "Yes. Quite all right. Clumsy of me."

She seemed capable only of short phrases as she fought for control of herself. She straightened and felt him step away.

"I'm sorry," she said. "You were saying something about dinner?"

The calmness in her voice pleased her, almost as much as her pounding pulse disturbed her.

He once again took her arm as they walked toward the big double doors which stood open. A welcoming glow of light showed a small entranceway behind. Still struggling for calm, Melisande tried to ignore the burning touch of his long fingers.

"This is called, very simply, The Inn. It's run by an immensely fat Spanish lady who is very fond of English romance novels. The house specialties are seafood and Spanish wines, both very good."

He smiled engagingly down at her, but Melisande could sense he was no more calm than she was as they walked into the restaurant.

"Señor Alex. Such time and you do not come! You can not be eating well! And last week the sea bass was so good! A pity!"

The vast good humor in the gravelly voice matched its owner. Melisande smiled, delighted by the spectacle of the elegant Alex Robeson being soundly kissed on the cheek by a lady who must have weighed at least two hundred and fifty pounds.

"Does that mean, Lourdes, that there's nothing fit to eat tonight?" Alex asked with a laugh as he straightened from the embrace. "And I promised Miss Merrick something special!"

The vast lady, a smile stretching her fat cheeks, turned to take Melisande's hand in her own plump, dimpled ones. Lourdes radiated welcome without saying a word, but Melisande found herself being studied by a pair of very shrewd eyes, and she suspected that because of her appearance with Alex Robeson, she was being considered very carefully.

"But of course! For this lovely lady we may find something tonight. The prawns, perhaps, will not be too bad. Do you like prawns, señorita?"

This last question was spoken with the utmost

concern as the vast lady continued to pat Melisande's hand absently. The slight crease in the broad brow under the severe hairdo showed the question was important and not mere polite chit-chat.

"I love prawns, and I'm sure yours must be the best. Alex told me your food was truly wonderful."

Melisande smiled, then felt an uncomfortable warmth begin to steal across her cheeks. She noticed that Alex immediately understood her sudden discomfiture and she felt an urge to give his shins a swift kick in return for the appreciative grin which lighted his dark face.

"But of course, that is true."

Lourdes nodded her head in recognition of an incontrovertible truth. Then she smiled suddenly and patted her ample sides.

"I enjoy good cooking too much. They *must* be the best!"

Lourdes laughed right along with Melisande while Alex smiled, the picture of amused, yet smug masculine self-satisfaction.

"Melisande, permit me to present Señora Lourdes Angelica Ruíz de Sanchez, the owner of one of the best restaurants in Rio," he said at last.

"The *best*, Señor Alex. The best! But come, you must have a good table. A very nice table for two."

Señora Sanchez turned and led them through an archway, past a long, dimly lit bar, and out onto an open patio scented by huge jasmine vines laden with the delicate, white flowers. The vines twisted up stone walls and across trellises, mixing with the brilliant colors of bougainvillea, bird-of-paradise, lilies, orchids, and other flowers and plants Melisande didn't even recognize.

"It's beautiful!" Melisande exclaimed, entranced by the richness and variety which surrounded her.

"After food, Lourdes likes gardening best, and she keeps a lot of gardeners very busy here." Alex stood beside her, sharing her enjoyment of the riot of color and the rich scents.

"But we can't keep her waiting," he continued. "Lourdes has chosen our table. Shall we?" He gestured toward a vine-covered arch beyond which Lourdes was making some last-minute arrangements to a small table for two.

Melisande stepped through the arch and onto a broad terrace on which several candlelit tables were scattered. The sweet scent of jasmine floated on the softly moving breeze, which carried with it the soft sighing of the sea below. Sheltered brass lanterns hung on the wall and the half-moon provided all the additional lighting necessary to create a scene of enchantment.

Nothing more than a soft murmur of voices came from the other tables, and Melisande had a fleeting mental picture of herself and Alex Robeson alone on the quiet terrace in the moonlight.

She glanced toward Alex. The light from the lanterns fell softly across her face, but left his a study of sharp planes, with shadows around the high cheekbones and in the hollows of the eyes.

Though his face told her nothing, his voice, when he spoke, was gentle with understanding of her reaction to the setting and the soft night around them.

"Like something out of a romance, I've always

thought. I suspect there may be kind fairies lurking about who are responsible for the place."

He stopped beside her, so close she had to tilt her head back to look into his eyes. Melisande smiled up at him, lost in the moment and his nearness, unconscious of the other diners or the impassive Lourdes.

He reached out a hand to touch her arm gently, then, as though shocked by the light contact, withdrew it abruptly and took a half step back away from her.

"The beauty of the terrace is entrancing, but don't forget we came here to dine."

His throat seemed constricted, and Melisande started, suddenly aware of the vast, immobile bulk of Lourdes standing beside the table and keenly observing them.

"The lady must sit here, where both the garden and the sea may be seen. To you, Señor Alex, I give the sea and the lady."

Her gesture as she showed them their respective places was graceful and somehow regal.

"I will send the headwaiter but I, myself, shall choose the wine. A very light, dry white to begin. I shall send it immediately."

The humor in her voice was gone, and the gravelly rasp had reasserted itself now that the talk had returned to the important matter of food. She turned and, despite her bulk, disappeared quietly into the garden.

Suddenly, and with what she realized was a total lack of dignity, Melisande giggled. She put her fingers to her lips to stifle the sound, but her eyes twinkled wickedly at her companion.

"I know it's rude," she whispered, "but when she began to talk about the wine, I just realized how cavalierly I've been treating the subject of dinner."

Alex choked, then quickly clapped his own hand over his mouth, hiding the spreading grin that suddenly appeared there. Like Melisande's, his eyes danced, and the crinkling laugh lines at their edges gave his usually sober face an almost boyish vitality.

"Naughty girl," he chided in a whisper. "We won't be allowed back if you misbehave so!"

"There's an imp among the fairies. I would *never* behave this way if it weren't for wicked influences!" Melisande tilted her nose in mock hauteur, compressing her lips tightly to suppress the grin that threatened.

"Wicked influences, is it?" His voice was still thick with laughter. "Wait until I've plied you with a few glasses of Lourdes's wine!"

"I'll have you know . . ." Melisande's retort was cut off by the noiseless appearance of an elegantly dressed and very sober-faced waiter.

The man bowed slightly to the two of them as they struggled to maintain a dignified calm in the face of so imposing an individual.

Melisande received her menu with what she hoped was aplomb, though she carefully avoided looking across the table at her companion.

Alex's voice, when he spoke, had an odd tightness to it, but regained its usual fluidity as he and the waiter, Carlos, discussed the evening's specialties in the soft Brazilian Portuguese.

"Do you have any preferences?" Alex asked Melisande. "Or would you prefer to be guided by Carlos, who can choose the best of the best?"

"I trust Carlos completely, but . . ." She paused, her eyes twinkling.

"But?" prodded Alex.

"But since Lourdes says the prawns are not *too* bad, I wonder if we shouldn't order those?"

Melisande's lips compressed tightly to stifle another giggle as she thought of the imposing lady's serious manner of considering the possibility of the prawns being, perhaps, edible.

Alex's manful struggle to suppress the laughter that threatened almost started Melisande giggling again, but she was saved from further indiscretion by the arrival of the wine steward with a well-chilled bottle of wine. He was closely followed by a young man bearing a wine cooler.

The ceremonious opening and tasting of the wine covered the dignified withdrawal of Carlos, and by the time the wine steward left them, Melisande had herself well under control.

"I'm sorry if I behaved badly," she said contritely. "I do usually try for decorum. Perhaps the place really *is* enchanted."

For a long moment silence, potent with unspoken emotion, hung between them; then Alex said quietly, "Perhaps it is. Enchanted."

His smile was warm, and Melisande felt again the dangerous glow within her. She quickly raised her wineglass.

"To Brazil and her people."

Alex lifted his glass in recognition of her toast, then sipped thoughtfully.

"It's marvelous!" Melisande savored the delicate afterflavor of the golden liquid.

"Both Brazil and the wine." Alex lifted his glass again in salute. "And you," he added softly.

Melisande's hand trembled, and she ducked her head to avoid meeting his eyes. *Dangerous!* some voice within her kept shouting, but tonight, she knew, she would not listen to it.

"You were wise to choose the prawns," said the gravelly voice as Lourdes suddenly materialized beside them. "I have personally checked them, just to be sure, and they are quite acceptable."

The big woman studied them with indulgent satisfaction, and Melisande knew she had not missed the currents that flowed between Alex and herself. A benign smile creased the fat face, and Lourdes carefully placed a plate on the table between them.

"This I have prepared especially for you. It is good for a night such as tonight."

"It smells wonderful," said Melisande. "What is it?"

"Oysters."

"Oysters?" Alex's eyebrows shot upward. "Lourdes, have I told you lately how wicked you can be?"

Melisande detected a struggle between amusement and irritation in his voice, and was grateful the darkness hid her rising blush. Someday she would have to master that betraying heat; it had become too much of an embarrassing handicap lately.

"Why should you consider me wicked, Señor Alex? We have very fine oysters today. I have merely prepared them for a favored customer. But if you continue to call me wicked, perhaps I shall no longer have you as a customer."

Lourdes's chin lifted in majestic indignation, but

even Melisande could see she was enjoying her little joke. As Lourdes turned and walked away as quietly as she had come, Alex tried to apologize.

"Don't," said Melisande. "I like her very much." She grinned in spite of her blushes. "Shouldn't you try the oysters?"

The oysters were as good as promised, and the humor in their offering eased the tension that both Melisande and Alex were struggling against.

They talked of trivialities, of their likes and dislikes, their childhoods and their families. They would fall silent, wrapped in the enchantment of the night, but the silence was welcome and friendly, not strained.

The prawns were delicious, and they savored the subtle flavors of wine and food, talking as diners will of the foods they loved and the restaurants they had known.

The waiters were silent and good at what they did; Melisande scarcely noticed their comings and goings.

For her the universe had narrowed to only the two of them, wrapped in the warm Brazilian night and serenaded by the restless sea and the soft breeze. If the present was all she had, then she was determined to enjoy it to the fullest and not permit doubts to mar the perfection of the moment.

FIFTEEN

They were lingering over their coffee, and Melisande was laughing at Alex's recounting of an escapade from his childhood when Lourdes reappeared beside them.

"My garden table has been set with some glasses and some of my own liqueurs. You know the way, Señor Alex. Why do you not take your lady and listen to the sea up close?"

Alex put a protective arm around Melisande and led her slowly down a long stone stairway illuminated by soft lights set into the stone wall at one side. At the end of the stairway lay a hidden bower cut into the hillside.

If the terrace was enchanted, Lourdes's garden belonged to the fairy queen. They could see and hear nothing of the restaurant above them. Below them the sea washed around the sharp rocks, soothing, yet stirringly primeval. Hidden lights provided a soft glow of warm yellow against the dark stone and candles flickered in their silver and crystal holders on a table set for two.

Alex lifted a cut-glass decanter filled with an amber liquid and smiled at Melisande.

"Lourdes will never tell me what's in this, but it

can only be the nectar of the gods, it's so good. Would you like a glass?"

Melisande could only nod. As she took the delicate crystal liqueur glass from him, her fingers brushed against his and heat suddenly raced through her. She trembled at the fire he stirred so easily, and yet she gloried in it, as well.

She took a sip of the delicate, haunting liqueur and sighed with pleasure.

"But you're wrong, you know," she said softly. "It can't be made by the gods, because this is fairyland."

"And this is a Brazilian summer night," said Alex softly, coming to stand beside her. "Can it be enchanted even if it isn't midsummer?"

Melisande swayed closer to him, her green eyes widening with unspoken promise. "It can if you're in fairyland."

Alex's eyes met hers, and she heard the sudden intake of his breath. Without speaking, he put his glass on the table, then took hers and set it beside his before turning back to her.

"I thought you didn't believe in fairy tales?" His breath was warm on her cheek.

"I don't," she said softly as his lips came even closer. "I wouldn't, except that I'm here with you and—"

She had no chance to finish. The kiss was as enchanted as the garden around them. There was passion in it, passion that made her strain to meet the urgent demands she felt in his lips, passion that crushed her against him, and passion in the trembling hardness of his body.

But there was also infinite sweetness, as though

the moment had been touched by magic and transformed. *Magically transformed*, Melisande thought, and she knew that nothing, now, would ever be the same.

Alex lifted his head at last to look deep into Melisande's eyes, but he kept her tightly wrapped in his arms while one hand gently caressed the now-tangled mass of hair that swept her shoulder.

Beneath her hand, pressed tightly against his body by their closeness, Melisande could feel the rapid, uneven rise and fall of his chest, and she knew a swift exultation that she, Melisande Merrick, had the power to move him as he moved her.

"If this is fairyland," he said softly, "then you are the chief enchantress."

He ran a gentle fingertip along the soft lines of her mouth, swollen now after the demanding torment of his kisses, across her high cheekbones and the delicate arch of her eyebrows.

"Perhaps it's your emerald eyes. Emeralds have always had magic powers."

"I don't have emerald eyes," Melisande responded, turning slightly to kiss that tantalizing finger that stroked her skin.

"You do tonight." He gently kissed the lid of first one eye, then the other. "Magic emerald eyes."

Melisande closed her eyes with a contented sigh and laid her head against his chest. Here in the lower garden, the breeze off the sea was cooler, but wrapped in his arms with the warm, hard length of his body against hers she felt safe and protected. The outside world with all its doubts and pains couldn't reach her while he held her.

"God, Melisande, you're so sweet." His voice was

muffled by the heavy mane of her hair, for his cheek rested on the top of her head.

Gently, enticingly, his hand caressed her back, the soft skin of her bare shoulder, tentatively dropped to her hip, then rose along the column of her spine. Where he touched her he left a rising heat that spread inexorably. Melisande felt her body lift in response, straining against his as he aroused the smoldering fire that lay at the very center of her being, fanning the flames with his touch as they rose higher and higher within her.

"Alex!" she cried, lifting her face to his, unsure if her cry were a plea for release, or a call from her soul to the answering depths of his.

It didn't matter. Nothing mattered except his lips, crushing down on hers, and his arms, tightening about her in their mutual straining to become one.

His lips left hers as he raised his head, groaning, to stare at her with eyes transformed into dark pools by his desire. His fingers were brutally laced through the hair at the base of her neck, forcing her head back, her neck arched, so that she couldn't escape him if she'd wanted to.

She didn't want to. The aching hunger in her eyes told him that more clearly than mere words could have done. For an endless moment they hung suspended, caught by their unspoken need for each other; then a gasping, shuddering cry escaped him and Alex bent once more to meet her eager mouth.

Only at the point when they would have irrevocably tipped into complete abandonment did Alex at last wrench away from her. Dazed, Melisande swayed toward him with an incoherent protest. The large, strong hands that had caressed her until her body burned and ached and trembled now clasped her arms painfully, holding her away.

"No, my love, no." His voice quavered as he gasped for breath, fighting for control. "I'm only human. Not here."

There was no coldness in him now, Melisande knew. He wasn't rejecting her, only struggling with himself and his desire for her. Something within her sang at the knowledge of his need, and her bruised and swollen lips lifted in a smile of unutterable happiness.

Her own body ached with an answering need, and her breathing came as raggedly as his, but the joy within her made her content to await fulfillment, knowing the waiting would only make that fulfillment infinitely sweeter.

Uncertainly, Alex stepped back without taking his eyes from her, then reached for his glass and swallowed the contents in one convulsive gulp.

"We can go out the back way," he said. "Lourdes won't mind."

Melisande said nothing, only smiled in happy acceptance of whatever he chose. He stepped back to her, stretching out his hand in a futile effort to straighten the tumbled, shining hair he'd disarranged.

She could feel his fingers tremble slightly as they brushed against the still-fevered flesh at the back of her neck.

She laughed softly as she moved to fit herself against his side, her arm about his waist while his arm wrapped hesitantly about her shoulders.

From the safety of his side, she twisted to look up into his face.

"Pirates always seem to know the back ways," she murmured, "even in fairyland."

They said nothing in the car. Melisande was content to go wherever he wanted to take her, but she hoped that tonight he wanted to take her to the moon and back. The sensual abandon of the ball and her heated response to his every touch, every word, had shattered the last barrier that she'd erected between them.

Yet he would have to be the one to make the first move. She was not after his wealth or social position, and she didn't want to do anything to make him think she was. All she wanted was Alex, and she wanted him in every way she could get him.

Now she sat watching his strong profile, lighted every now and then by the passing cars. Her hand lay on his thigh—it was as far as she'd dared venture. To her relief, he'd smiled at her first tentative gesture, then clasped his warm, strong hand over hers, holding her against him. She thrilled to the movement of the hard muscle beneath her fingers. He didn't glance at her very often, but she knew, somehow, that it was because he feared the tension that flared between them every time their eyes met, and she gloried in the knowledge.

Every once in a while, after shifting gears, he would lift his hand to brush her cheek or caress the length of her thigh, so close to his own, before letting it drop back to cover hers. His hands were beautifully shaped, with long, sensitive fingers that drew her thoughts in dangerous directions. She tried not to think about his fingers.

When he at last drove into the underground parking lot of a tall building in one of Rio's most luxurious residential areas, Melisande knew, without
being told, that he'd brought her to his own apartment. He'd brought her home. Her heart skipped
a beat at the thought, then settled into a quick,
eager rhythm that betrayed her eagerness . . . and
her fears.

They rode up in the elevator without speaking,
arms about each other in a strangely hesitant,
temptingly intimate embrace. Only when they'd entered the penthouse apartment did Alex turn away
from her to shut the door while Melisande stood
looking about her.

The entry opened directly onto the apartment's
living room. Long, plump leather sofas invited
guests to sit and make themselves comfortable,
while scattered table lamps provided a soft yellow
glow that illuminated the graceful modern furniture
and the stunning art that hung on the walls. As in
her apartment, the far living-room wall was all glass,
opening onto a wide balcony, but instead of the sea
Melisande saw the glittering sweep of Rio at night,
scarcely dimmed by the glass or the reflections of
the lamps.

Against the backdrop of the city, the apartment
was a serene, welcoming refuge. The room was masculine without being hard and far more intimate
than she had expected. Like the man himself, here
was a warm, sophisticated center shut off from the
world by high walls and a door through which only
a very few could pass.

Melisande felt, rather than heard, Alex come to

her across the heavy carpet. She turned to him, tremblingly expectant.

He stopped a few paces away. An expression of sudden uncertainty crossed his face. His hands came up in an imploring gesture, then dropped to his sides. He started to speak, but closed his mouth without saying anything.

It was, she thought, as though he had come to the end of whatever he'd planned and now didn't quite know what came next. The notion was absurd, of course, yet she knew, suddenly, that it was up to her to make the next move, that he would leave the ultimate decision of how this night would end to her, and to her alone. The thought made her feel a little dizzy, a little frightened, and very, very eager.

"Oh, Alex!" she said softly, and threw her arms about him. Though he still made no move to touch her, she buried her face against the fine fabric of his jacket, forcing him to bend down to catch her plea.

"Love me, Alex. Please."

Alex froze, uncertain that he had really heard the words he'd wanted to hear, the words that had teased at him ever since he'd seen her walking across her living room, coming through the light . . . to him.

Dinner had been exquisite—and exquisitely tormenting. The ride here had been just plain tormenting. The intimate, enclosed space of the Mercedes had been alive with a thousand possibilities and unspoken promises. Her hand on his thigh, the way the lights from the street outlined her delicate profile, hiding as much as they revealed, the teasing subtlety of her perfume, and the soft rustle of silk as she moved—all had combined to tease his senses and arouse dangerous thoughts and even more dangerous desires.

He'd managed to restrain himself to an occasional caress, a glancing look, but it hadn't been easy. He'd really wanted to bring the Mercedes to a screeching stop, right there in the middle of the street, then pull her into his arms so he could ravage that soft, sweet mouth of hers. He'd also wanted to gun the Mercedes and burn the roads between them and his apartment. He'd managed to keep from doing either, but it hadn't been easy.

Now she was here, his for the taking, and to his amazement, he found himself suddenly reluctant to make the first move.

He wanted her, but he wanted her to want him in return. He wanted her to ache as he ached, burn as he burned. He wanted her to admit that the attraction between them was something they would ignore only at their peril.

And then she'd thrown herself into his arms and whispered four magic words: *Love me, Alex. Please.*

The words shattered the last of his restraint. All the tension that had hung between them, all the doubts and fears that had held them back, disappeared in the sensual firestorm that engulfed them.

With a choking cry, he wrapped his arms around her in a crushing embrace.

"Melisande. My God!" he said, and claimed her mouth with his.

A moment passed, or an eternity, Melisande wasn't sure which, while the world was forgotten. And then she found herself being carried in his arms through a dark hallway and into the pale, golden light of his bedroom. Melisande was vaguely aware of the vast bed as he gently, worshipfully lowered her onto it, but when he started to draw away, she tightened her arms about his neck with a cry.

"Don't leave me!"

He made no effort to free himself, but knelt before her. His gaze locked with hers. His hands were warm and strong and gentle on her arms.

"I won't leave you," he said softly. "I couldn't."

He bent his head to press a kiss on the point of her shoulder, then another and another along the line of her collarbone.

She closed her eyes as her head fell back, opening her to his mouth. His seeking lips burned across her bare skin. His hands roamed her body, caressing, teasing her with his demanding search for the union they both craved. Melisande felt cool air against her fevered flesh and the brush of silk as her dress fell to her waist.

She heard his shuddering intake of breath and opened her eyes to find his hungry gaze upon her golden, naked body.

"Like silk," he said, as if in prayer, and brushed the tip of one finger along the curve of her breast, then down to the peak of her nipple. "Like warm silk."

He bent again and took her in his mouth. His tongue rasped against her skin, warm and moist and rough. He nipped at the sensitive peak, then sucked.

She couldn't help it. She cried out and arched toward him, offering herself in mindless, aching response. He drew back and she cried out again, this

time in protest, but he pulled away in spite of it
and rose to his feet, drawing her with him.

A moment he loomed above her, eyes blazing and
hot with wanting her, and then he dropped his gaze
to her waist, fumbling for the fastenings that still
held her dress in place.

Melisande stood there, hands lifted at her sides,
out of his way, and watched him. And as she
watched, excitement swelled within her, excitement
and a sense of power that was unlike anything she
had ever known.

"Here," she said, and heard the laughter and the
joy bubbling up in her voice. "Like this."

With one deft twitch, she unfastened the last
hook and let the dress fall away from her. It
dropped to the floor, billowing at her feet in a
silken, radiant shimmer of color, leaving her clad
in her lacy panties and nothing more.

She hadn't had many such experiences before,
but when she had, she'd always found it embarrassing to be like this, scarcely covered and vulnerable,
open to another's view.

Not now. Now she stood in her silky bit of clothing and gloried in her body and the power it possessed to make Alex want her.

And he did want her. If she'd had any lingering
doubts about that, they vanished under his heated
gaze. He wanted her just as she wanted him. *Her,*
not just her body. Of that she was certain. And with
that certainty came a matching certainty that she
had fallen in love with him in spite of all her firm
intentions not to.

"You're so . . . beautiful," he said. It might have
been a prayer. "Beautiful."

"Like a jewel?" she teased, savoring his hunger, yet shaken by the knowledge that loving him had made her vulnerable in ways she had never been before.

He shook his head. "More beautiful than that. So alive and real and warm."

He stretched out his hand to trace the length of her arm all the way down to her hips, then around to the top edge of her panties. The slight contact was almost imperceptible, yet it was enough to set her trembling. He flattened his hand on her belly, then slid it up to mold the curve of her waist.

"You are . . . glorious," he murmured. "No jewel can match that, ever."

"And you are still clothed." She tugged at the end of his tie.

His mouth curved in a wide grin as he slid his hand around to the small of her back and pulled her against him. "You can easily remedy that little problem . . . if you like."

Melisande laughed and slid her hand up to the knot of his tie. "I like."

She wasn't sure which was more erotic, having Alex undress her or his letting her undress him.

The tie and jacket were easy. So were the buttons on his shirt and the cuff links at its wrists. She tugged his shirt off and flung it atop his discarded jacket. Her fingertips tingled from brushing against his skin as she'd worked, but the feel of the soft hair on his chest when she ran her hand across that hard-muscled expanse set her whole body to tingling.

"Don't stop there," he said, and tugged her hands down to his belt.

She didn't. She didn't linger over the task, either. The need to see him, to feel his naked body against hers, and to take him deep inside her was almost overwhelming.

Her fingers trembled as she fumbled with the buckle of his belt and the fastener at his waistband. After one quick tug, his zipper nearly sprang open of its own accord, yet rather than explore behind it, she knelt and, one by one, tugged off his shoes and socks.

It was Alex's impatience that foiled her erotic plans. With an explosive curse, he pulled her to her feet, then stripped her panties from her, immediately ridding himself of the last of his own clothes.

Her inarticulate protest was lost in a moan of pleasure as he lowered her down on the bed and covered her body with his own.

One wild kiss as their bodies strained for union. And then he was in her and the fire of their joining wrenched a groan from somewhere deep inside him.

"Melisande," he said, half-whisper, half-plea. *"Melisande."*

She heard no more, for everything was consumed in sensation and the fire that fused them into one.

The bedside lamp still burned when Alex awoke shortly after dawn. With an effort of will, he rolled onto his elbow, then stretched out to snap it off. Behind him, half-hidden under the tumbled sheets and with her head buried in a mound of pillows, Melisande lay on her side, lost in sleep. Her only response to his movement was to curl toward him with a murmured, unintelligible protest.

Careful not to wake her, he sank back onto the bed and rolled over to face her. There wasn't much to see except a tangled spill of hair across the pillow that obscured most of her face, yet revealed her shoulder where it poked out of the sheets. Her bare arm was tucked tight against her body, her hand protectively curled up under her breast, the fingers curved toward her palm.

Asleep like this, naked beneath the tumbled sheets, she looked sweetly innocent and deliciously wanton, all at the same time. His body couldn't help but respond.

With his free hand, he traced the smooth line of her shoulder and upper arm, the angle of the elbow, the sweep of her forearm down to the wrist. He stopped just at the edge of the thick pad of flesh and muscle beneath her thumb.

Mound of Venus it was called he remembered vaguely. Or was that another, more intimate mound? He couldn't remember. Not that it mattered.

He ran the tip of one fingernail over the soft mound, following its joining with her thumb. He traced the inside curve of her thumb, then back down, over the mound and into the cup of her palm. Her fingers twitched, then stilled.

Gently, still with just the tip of his fingernail, he stroked her palm from the center to the pad of flesh beneath one finger, then to the next finger, and the next.

Melisande muttered something in her sleep and jerked her hand away.

Intrigued with this new game, Alex leaned closer

to lightly blow in her ear. His efforts brought another sleepy mutter of irritation as she vaguely swatted at the annoyance, then burrowed deeper into her pillows.

"Melisande." It was no more than a whisper.

"Humph?"

"Melisande?"

One eyelid fluttered, then slowly opened. It took her a moment to focus as she slowly came awake. "Alex?"

He grinned. "You were expecting someone else?"

She blinked, took a deep breath, and shifted on the pillow for a better view. A sleepy, satisfied smile curved her lips. "Good morning."

Desire shot through him. "Is it?"

She nodded. The slight motion dislodged a heavy lock of her hair so that it tumbled across her cheek like a thick, shiny ribbon.

Alex carefully tucked it back behind her ear.

Her smile widened. "Have you been awake long?"

"No." He pushed back the mass of tumbled hair, savoring the weight and the silky feel of it, then let his hand shape the curve of her shoulder. Her skin was warm to the touch, soft.

If she looks as good the morning after as she looked the night before, you know she's the one.

The thought hit with startling force. His grip on her shoulder tightened.

Melisande looked even more desirable in the morning than she'd looked last night, and last night he'd thought he would explode from wanting her.

"Are you one of those ambitious types who leaps out of bed at the crack of dawn so he can get right to work?" she asked.

It might have been an innocent question, but there was nothing innocent about the glint in her eye or the way she threaded her fingers through the hair on his chest.

"Not this morning." he said, conscious of the sudden tightness in his voice.

"Good." She let her hand drift lower.

Alex's breath caught somewhere in the middle of his chest. Right then he decided there wasn't a chance in hell that he was going to leap out of bed.

SIXTEEN

"Now this," said Melisande with satisfaction, "is the right way to start a morning." She lifted her glass of freshly squeezed orange juice in a teasing toast.

Alex's housekeeper, who had arrived earlier loaded down with string bags filled with fresh fruit and bread, had laid out breakfast on the small table at one side of the apartment's rooftop patio. Jasmine half-buried the latticework frame overhead, shading them from the bright morning sun and perfuming the air with the scent of its delicate white blossoms. The spot offered a magnificent view of Rio and the hills around it, but as far as Melisande was concerned, the best-looking thing around was the man seated across the table from her.

Alex laughed. "The view, you mean?"

Melisande's grip on the glass tightened. His laughter warmed her, thick and rich and strong as the coffee in her cup.

She shook her head. "Not just the view. Everything. This meal. The morning. You." Her gaze locked with his. "Us."

He stilled suddenly as though she'd struck him. For an instant, she wondered if she'd presumed too much; then his mouth once more curved upward in a smile.

He lifted his own glass and touched its rim to hers. "To mornings," he said, and drained the glass.

Melisande sipped her juice more slowly, shaken by that fleeting doubt. Surely she hadn't been mistaken. The look in his eyes when she'd awakened, the gentle, lazy, passionate lovemaking that had followed—surely she hadn't misunderstood what they all meant. Had she?

A moment ago, she would have sworn that what she saw in Alex's eyes mirrored what he must see in hers—excitement, desire. Love.

Love, most of all. Foolish or mad or misguided she might be, but she had fallen irrevocably in love with Alex Robeson.

The thought made her tug nervously at the collar of the terry bathrobe Alex had loaned her, pulling it closer around her. The slight gesture drew his gaze downward an instant before he took a hasty sip of coffee.

Melisande smiled and felt some of the sudden tension within her ease. He'd offered her the garment when hunger had finally driven them from his bed. Her dress, revealingly crumpled after having been cavalierly tossed aside last night, hadn't seemed quite the thing to wear for breakfast, yet she found the oversized robe with its faint, lingering scent of him a far more potent reminder of what they'd shared than the dress would ever have been.

"So," he said, "what do you want to do today? Go for a drive along the coast? Up into the hills? Maybe see a few of the sites you haven't hit so far?"

She almost said that she wanted to go back to

bed, with him. Just the thought of a lazy day spent making love to Alex was enough to set her blood to racing. The words were on the tip of her tongue when she remembered that none of it was possible.

"I can't," she said, and knew he could hear the disappointment in her voice. "Catalina finally managed to wangle an invitation for me to look over a private collection of old journals and documents from the period I'm studying. The lady who owns the collection doesn't often open it to scholars, so I don't dare lose this opportunity. As it is, I'm sure there will be far more than I can possibly get through in an afternoon. If I'm to have a chance of being invited back, I'd better not be late on the first visit."

Was that, she wondered, an expression of disappointment on his face? She couldn't really tell.

All he said was, "When?"

"I'm meeting Catalina at ten, which means," she added with regret, "that I probably ought to get moving. I have to go home, change, gather my things . . ."

She'd almost said she had to shower, but she had already had a morning shower. Two actually, since the first had ended when Alex had slipped in to share it with her.

The memory made her heart miss a beat and brought a flush to her cheeks. This time she had no difficulty reading Alex's expression; he was remembering the shower, too.

"I'll join you," he said. "May I? If you have all that much work to get through, it can't hurt to have another translator along to help, can it?"

"No, it can't," said Melisande, hoping she didn't

look too eager. Not when she still wasn't exactly sure of what he was thinking, what he was feeling.

Alex scowled at the page in front of him. The paper was yellow and brittle with age, the once-black ink now a pale brown that was hard to read in the shadowed room. His shoulders hurt from sitting hunched over for so long, and his eyes ached from straining to make out the words that women now long dead had written over a century and a half ago.

He sat back, squeezing his shoulders together to ease the tension in his muscles, and glanced down at the intent figure at the other end of the battered old table. When Melisande had walked in here a few hours back, she'd come as close to squealing with delight as any grown woman he'd ever known. He, on the other hand, had taken one look at the room, crowded from floor to ceiling with old books and crudely bound journals and odd bits of old paper, and had damned near groaned out loud.

At the time, he'd wondered if he could possibly back out of his promise to help, then had decided it was far too late for that. Now he wished he'd found the courage to do it.

Yet in spite of his weariness and physical discomfort, he had to admit there was a certain fascination in looking at a world now past through the eyes of the women who had known it firsthand. Weary, overworked, and often discouraged, they'd poured their dreams and fears and hopes onto the pages of their private journals and the letters they'd sent home. They hadn't written for anyone except them-

selves and the friends and family they had left behind, yet their words reached across the years to
touch him with unsparing truths.

For the first time he understood—really, truly understood—the fascination this work had for Melisande. The owner of this collection had sensed it,
as well. Charmed by Melisande's enthusiasm and a
substantial dollop of deliberate charm from him,
she had given leave for Melisande to linger as long
as she liked and to return whenever she wanted.

"It's not something I usually do, you know," she
had said in her quavery, old-woman's voice, looking
around at the dusty, overburdened shelves. "My husband collected them, and he was very protective of
his things. But I'm getting old and perhaps . . ."

She'd let the words die away; then she'd blinked
and patted Melisande on the shoulder and said,
"You take your time, dear. Ring for Anna if you
need anything. She'll get it for you."

And then she had gone away and left the three
of them, him and Melisande and Catalina, to what
seemed like the impossible task of sorting through
the material in the room.

Alex knew he'd have been lost on his own, but
Melisande and Catalina had plunged in eagerly.
They soon had a pile set aside for him to sort
through and larger piles for themselves. Melisande
had claimed anything in English, of course. The
bulk of the collection was in Portuguese and Spanish, so that was divided between Catalina and him.
Anything in German went straight to Catalina.

Alex's job was to scan the stuff they brought him,
setting aside any personal accounts dating from the
nineteenth century for their inspection. He'd

started off determined to deal with the material as efficiently as he dealt with the mounds of paper that came across his desk at work, but it wasn't long before he found himself caught up in his reading.

Nonetheless, despite the fascinating stories buried in these old papers, there were limits, and he'd just reached his. He wasn't reading another page until he'd had a cup of coffee, at least. A glass of good wine would be even better.

The thought of wine brought a regretful sigh. That was undoubtedly asking too much, though the coffee shouldn't be hard to come by. All he had to do was go to the door and shout for Anna. Melisande would probably never even notice.

He'd swear she would have forgotten his presence entirely if he hadn't taken care to remind her of it from time to time. She'd scarcely raised her head when Catalina had had to leave, and then only to smile a vague good-bye an instant before turning back to the stuff in front of her.

Well, he'd had enough of it, and so had she. She just didn't know it yet.

With sudden decision, he shoved aside the pile of papers he'd been reading and leaned back in his chair, locking his hands over his head and stretching to work out the lingering stiffness. Melisande didn't so much as blink, let alone look up from her notes.

An odd sort of feeling stabbed at him, something almost like resentment. He could understand her being immersed in work—he got that way himself at times—but forgetting him entirely was going just a little too far.

The thought made him frown, then blink in

guilty amazement. Absurd as it seemed, he was jealous of her work, of the way it dragged her attention away from him.

The thought bothered him. He wasn't a jealous man. Never had been, never would be. And what did it matter, anyway? In a few months, she would be heading back to New York and he'd still be here with more than enough work to keep two men busy.

He didn't much like that thought, either, which bothered him even more. New York was a hell of a long way away.

He shook his head and abruptly leaned forward to slap his palms on the table. This wasn't like him. Not like him at all. What he needed was coffee. Or, better yet, to get out of here altogether and take Melisande with him. If, that is, he could pry her out of her beloved books.

He studied her as she frowned at the journal she was reading, then snatched up her pencil—he'd learned that working around old documents with a pen was considered a no-no of the highest order; accidental pencil marks could be erased, pen marks couldn't—and began writing in her thick notebook.

It was no wonder she was so nearsighted, he thought. A tempting little crease appeared right above the bridge of her nose when she peered at the fading print. It was as if she were determined that not a word would escape her, determined to wrench the lost secrets out of the fading words in those old journals and letters and find Truth with a capital *T*. Like a knight searching for the Holy Grail, he thought, then shook off the fanciful notion.

With a wry grin, he shoved back his chair. The

sound of it grating on the old parquet floor finally roused her from her trance. She looked up, a vaguely puzzled, inquiring expression on her face.

"Enough," he said firmly, rising and walking down the length of the table to her. "The sun's gone, and these old lamps aren't much use to anyone. You'll go blind if you work any longer."

She blinked, laughed, and, pulling off her glasses, leaned back in her chair, then scrubbed at her eyes with her fingers.

"It's a bad habit," she admitted. "I get so involved I completely forget about the time."

"And me."

"Not you!"

He cocked his head and arched his eyebrows in exaggerated disbelief.

That made her laugh again. The sound was sweet as syrup in the dusty, crowded room.

"All right, maybe I do. A little," she admitted. "But I forget about everyone when I'm working. Everyone except the people whose papers I'm reading."

"They're very real to you, aren't they?"

She let her gaze drop to the documents scattered across the table in front of her. "Yes. Yes, they are. When I read what they've written, I—I feel as if I know them, as if I'm there with them, experiencing whatever it is they're experiencing." She shrugged, embarrassed. "I suppose that sounds absurd."

"No." He held out his hand. "But staying here all night certainly does."

With an embarrassed little laugh she let him pull her to her feet. When he drew her against him, she simply leaned into him, sliding her arms around his

waist and letting her head rest on his chest. He
kneaded her shoulders, the back of her neck, down
her spine, and wondered at the protective feeling
that washed through him as he did.

"Why don't you leave your things here and come
back tomorrow?" he said. "It would be easier—"

She shook her head. The soft bun brushed
against his chin, silken and cool. "I wish I could,
but I have an appointment tomorrow morning and
another the day after. Catalina didn't think I'd be
allowed more than the one visit, so I didn't
plan . . ."

Her words trailed off into another sigh. "There's
so much here, so much still to do. I feel as if I've
barely touched the surface. No, I *know* I have."

Abruptly, she pulled free of his arms and turned
to frown at the jumble of papers and leather-bound
journals. She held out her hands in an encompass-
ing, palms-up gesture of helpless frustration, then
let them drop to her side. "If only I could stay a
little longer."

It was his turn to frown. "So why don't you? The
apartment's no problem. You can—" He stopped,
startled. He'd almost said she could live with him.
"We can find you another place to live if the
owner's coming back."

"It's not that. Or not just that," she said, her gaze
still fixed on the papers. There was a note of strain
in her voice that hadn't been there a moment before, a hesitancy in her manner that surprised him
almost as much as the thought of having her live
with him.

"What, then?"

She shook her head, deliberately not looking at

him, and fussed with her notes in a halfhearted attempt to straighten them. "Nothing."

Alex pulled her around to face him. "Come on. You can tell me. What is it?"

Yet even as he pushed the issue, he wasn't at all sure he wanted to hear the answer. Her sudden change of mood troubled him. He experienced an uncomfortable, almost childish twinge of resentment that the topic should have come up at all, yet under that resentment was the very real and, to him, very frightening knowledge that he didn't want to think about her leaving. Not now, perhaps not ever. And that thought troubled him more than all the rest put together.

"What?" he said again, and forced an encouraging smile onto his face.

She refused to look at him. "I—I don't have the money to stay longer, Alex. Even if I had an apartment and my university would extend my sabbatical, I don't have the money to stay."

"Oh," said Alex, and his hands fell away from her shoulders as if of their own volition. He stepped back, not even half a step, but it felt like much, much more. "I see."

Melisande peered up at him through her lashes, suddenly miserable. Why had he asked in the first place? Why had he insisted?

She didn't want to think about leaving him, about the separation that lay ahead. That wasn't supposed to happen if you were in love. But he had persisted, and though his eyes had been kind and warm and his hold on her had been reassuringly gentle, she'd suddenly been afraid of the distance that lay between them—and the even greater distance there would be once she returned to New York.

That was why she'd said it was the money that prevented her from staying. Which was true enough, of course, but not entirely.

It had been the wrong thing to say. The words were scarcely out of her mouth when she'd seen his eyes grow cold and distant and had felt him stiffen. Then his hands had fallen away from her shoulders and he stepped back, and she knew she'd made a mistake.

But she couldn't, not for the life of her, tell just where or when.

There was a stiffness between them as Melisande gathered up her notes and Alex tidied the jumble of books and papers strewn across the table. Every time she looked up she opened her mouth to speak, to explain, but each time she shut it again, uncertain.

He finished as quickly as she did. "Ready?"

She nodded and forced a smile. "Ready. You were right," she added as he held the door for her. "I hadn't realized how late it had gotten."

"That seems to be a habit of yours." This time when he smiled, his smile seemed softer, not so stiff and forced.

It wasn't much, but it was enough to ease at least a little of the tension in her. "It is. Just ask anyone who knows me. My colleagues in New York take great pleasure in keeping track of the number of times I've almost been locked into the library at the end of the day."

"Next time I'm in New York, I'll be sure to ask."

He said it casually, as if it were the easiest thing in the world to do, and Melisande could have sworn the sun came back up when he did.

How could she have been so blind? Of *course* he went to New York. Often. Robeson and Company was one of the world's great jewelers. They had offices in London, Paris, Rome—she couldn't remember all of the cities where they had shops. But she did remember New York.

And she didn't have to leave Rio yet, in any case. There was still time for . . . everything.

She smiled and hitched the strap of her overstuffed briefcase higher on her shoulder. He'd offered to carry it and she'd refused, but suddenly it didn't seem nearly as heavy as it had just a few minutes ago. Not anywhere near as heavy.

He couldn't figure Melisande out. One minute she was as stiff and uncomfortable as he was, the next she was smiling and cheerful as a woman who'd just been told her lottery ticket had come through a winner.

Well, almost a winner. He took his eyes off the insane traffic that was Rio on a normal day and glanced over at her. She was turned away from him, watching something out the side window of the Mercedes. Her hands were lightly clasped in her lap, their long, shapely fingers relaxed, still with the confident calm that was one of the things he liked best about her.

From this angle, he could see the delicate lines of brow and cheek and chin and the graceful curve of her throat, but he couldn't see the expression in her eyes or the set of her mouth.

He didn't really need to. She was a little more subdued now, but at least she wasn't as stiff and distant as she'd been there in that old study.

As stiff as they'd both been, he reminded himself, turning his attention back to the traffic.

What had he been thinking of? She wasn't after his money. He knew that. That wasn't the way Melisande Merrick operated.

His grip on the wheel tightened. He just couldn't help it, he admitted to himself. His withdrawal had been an automatic response, one he'd learned long ago and had had far too much practice with since. Trouble was, that instinctive reaction had never bothered him before. Certainly not like now.

Maybe Maria was right. Maybe he did need to rethink things. Find the right woman, get married.

Just the thought was enough to make him tense. And yet . . .

Because he couldn't help himself, he glanced at Melisande again. To his surprise, she was watching him. As their eyes met, her mouth lifted in the unconsciously erotic smile he was coming to know so well.

The sight of it roused sharp, physical memories of the night before, of what they'd shared and the way she'd felt beneath him. He sucked in his breath and forced his attention back on the traffic.

"I don't know how you stand it," she said. "I'd never have the nerve to drive in Rio traffic." She was staring at the crowded street in front of them. The angle offered a clearer view of her profile.

She could wear diamonds, he thought. Not every woman could. Not really. But Melisande could.

Emeralds would be better, though. Emeralds to match her eyes, deep green and brilliant.

He pushed the thought aside, shifted down for a red light. "You can say that when you live in New York?" he said, deliberately teasing.

She nodded. Even from the side, her smile was beautiful.

"I don't drive in New York. I don't even own a car. I wouldn't have the nerve to take it out of its parking spot, even if I could afford one. Which I can't," she added, turning the full force of her smile back on him.

Their eyes met, locked. Her smile faded, and that tiny little crease between her eyebrows suddenly appeared. She licked her lips nervously and heat shot through him.

This time, when the light turned to green, he had to wrench his gaze away.

He heard her draw in an unsteady breath. "There's an underground parking space that goes with my apartment," she said softly. "I've never used it and don't really know how to get to it, but if you could find it, you could use it. If you wanted to, that is," she added, more tentatively.

Her unspoken offer hung in the air between them. After last night, she had every right to expect that he would accept it. After his gaffe in that damned book-stuffed room, though, she wasn't nearly so sure of herself . . . or him.

And frankly, neither was he.

For a minute, he didn't say anything, just kept his attention on his driving and his hands on the wheel. Both of them. If the Mercedes people hadn't made such good steering wheels, he probably would have bent it.

With a deliberate effort of will, he forced himself to relax. "I'll find it," he said. "Just give me a chance."

She could have floated up to her apartment without benefit of an elevator. Melisande didn't think her feet had touched the ground since Alex had handed her out of the Mercedes. It was all she could do to keep herself from babbling. Excitement percolated through her veins like bubbles through champagne.

Her rational, analytical mind might tell her that she was rushing things, expecting too much, *wanting* too much, but her heart told her otherwise.

After twenty-five years of running things, she figured it was time her head gave way and let her heart take over. Just for a little while.

She glanced up to find him watching her, a faint, almost puzzled smile on his face. The smile might have worried her if it hadn't been for the look in his eyes. Hungry, wanting eyes with something else, something . . . wonderful lurking in their depths.

He opened his mouth, started to speak, but the dinging of the elevator announcing their arrival broke the spell.

"We're here," she said, a little breathlessly, and hurried out before he had a chance to realize how silly that sounded. She fumbled with the keys—he'd insisted on taking her briefcase with all her notes—

then threw the door open with a theatrical sweep of her arm and stepped back. "Please. Go in."

Instead of entering, Alex stopped in the middle of the open doorway just inches from her. He was so tall and so close that he loomed over her. His gaze, darker and hungrier than it had been just a few minutes earlier, pinned her to the painted frame.

"You're sure?"

All she could do was nod.

His lips parted on an indrawn breath as his hand brushed along the side of her face, conjuring heat.

"I'm glad," he said, and then he drew her in with him and closed the door behind them.

SEVENTEEN

The first storm of passion didn't last long, but it was followed by a slow and gentle loving that spun them to the heights, then set them free to drift slowly back to reality, sated and content.

Melisande sleepily studied the face so close beside hers on the pillow they shared, ran her finger across lips that were as swollen as her own. Alex's lips parted; he grasped her finger between his teeth and nibbled on it playfully.

"Hungry?" she asked.

His gaze locked with hers. "Not for food."

She feigned shock. "Surely you can't be hungry for more of . . . that?"

"No?" He shoved to one elbow. His gaze locked on her face as if he intended to memorize every line and curve and hollow of it.

"Well, not so soon, anyway," she said, and hoped that he was right and she was wrong on that particular point.

His gaze dropped. He lifted a wayward lock of hair that had spilled across the pillow between them. "You should wear your hair down all the time."

"So you've said, but you're not the one who has

to try to keep it in place against every little gust of wind that comes along."

"Who says you should keep it in place?" He tugged on the lock, then leaned forward to kiss her, a long, lingering, gentle kiss that roused an answering heat within her.

At the point where the kiss promised to turn into something more, he pulled back and sat up. "I have to go."

She shifted on the pillow, surprised. "Now?"

He bent to claim one last, swift kiss. "Now. I have a board meeting tomorrow morning, and work to do tonight to prepare for it."

"Oh." Disappointment shot through her, immediately followed by guilt. "I'm sorry. And here you've spent the whole day helping me when you—"

"Not the whole day." His gaze slid down the sheets that covered her naked body, then up again. "I had other . . . diversions, shall we say?"

Heat flooded her cheeks, yet she couldn't help beaming at the satisfaction she could hear in his voice. Satisfaction and something else, something far less easily defined, but all the more promising for it.

When he swung out of bed, she sat up, clutching the sheet to her breast. Already the bed felt bigger and emptier without him in it.

"Besides," he added, plucking his shirt off the bedroom chair on which he'd flung it earlier, "we'll be together again in a few hours. You haven't forgotten the Sebastians' invitation to go sailing tomorrow, have you?"

"No, but—" She bit her lip, embarrassed.

"But . . . ?"

"But I can't make love to you when we're having lunch with Maria and Stephen."

Laughter lighted his face. "No, you can't do that. Even Maria would be shocked."

"Then perhaps . . . lunch? If you're free?"

He shook his head. "I'll have to go straight to the harbor from the board meeting. I'm sorry."

So was she. The last thing she wanted to do was turn into a clinging, demanding female, however, so she had no choice but to put the best face on it that she could.

"Well, there'll be tomorrow evening," she said, forcing a cheerful note. "Or if not then, the next day. After all, we have 'Tomorrow, and tomorrow, and tomorrow.'"

"As I recall, that's not a very happy quotation." A frown creased his brow, so quickly she wasn't sure she'd seen it. "Better simply to enjoy the moments we have."

He was right, Melisande told herself. Better far to enjoy the moments they had, because he hadn't offered any guarantees and she knew it was far too soon for her to ask for them.

Still, logic didn't make things any easier when she heard the click of the lock as he quietly let himself out of the apartment a few minutes later. Not the least bit easier.

A faint hint of Melisande's perfume lingered in the close air of the Mercedes, Alex discovered. So faint, he might not have noticed it if he'd been able to quit glancing over at the empty passenger's seat as he drove, wishing she were there with him.

If it weren't for that damned board meeting—

He cut the thought off. The meeting had been scheduled for months. Bringing in senior people from Europe and the States so they could enjoy Carnaval and still get some work done was an unbreakable company tradition.

And he hadn't lied about the preparation he must do before the meeting, either. There was a stack of documents waiting on his desk at home and more data in his office, no doubt, though he hadn't been in lately to check. He'd been too engrossed in Melisande even to think about work.

If they were married—

The unexpected thought shook him so badly that he almost sideswiped a parked car.

Gut churning, Alex slammed to a stop at the side of the road. *Married?*

The idea was absurd. It was one thing to enjoy the company of a beautiful and intelligent woman like Melisande, quite another to fall in love and get married.

He stared out the windshield at the traffic rushing madly past. Where were they all going? he wondered vaguely, and knew the answer before the question was fully formed. At this hour of the night, most of them were going to their homes and families.

And where was he going? Back to an empty apartment and an even emptier bed.

He didn't much like the thought of it, which was strange, because he'd always been perfectly content with his life. *Perfectly content,* he told himself sternly, setting the Mercedes into motion.

So why did he have to fight the urge to turn around and drive back to Melisande's? And why, he wondered when he finally got home, did his apartment seem so strangely cold and unwelcoming, even after he'd snapped on every light in the place?

Grimly, Alex forced such thoughts from his mind. He had work to do and not all that much time to do it in if he was going to be prepared for tomorrow's meeting.

Choosing a bottle of wine at random from his small store, he poured himself a glass and gulped it down, then carried bottle and glass into the office he maintained at home.

The papers his secretary had sorted out for him were neatly stacked on the desk. His housekeeper had sharpened all his pencils just the way he liked them and had laid out his favorite pen beside a pristine pad of white notepaper.

Heedless of possible stains to the polished wood, he set the bottle of wine and the glass on the desk and deliberately drew the curtains so he wouldn't have his reflection staring back at him from the wall of glass.

An hour later, he'd worked his way through less than a quarter of the papers. If anybody asked him what any of them said, he'd be lost. Not one of them had made any sense, no matter how many times he'd read them.

Sighing in disgust, he refilled his glass from the half-empty bottle and started again with the document in front of him.

But this time he was going to take notes, he told himself. It was an old trick that had helped him focus on studying when in school, and it ought to work the same way now.

He managed to fill the first page of the notepad

with almost illegible scribbles, but by the second he found himself doing what he often did at times of stress—doodling jewelry designs across the crisp white paper.

The rough sketches crowded the page in a tangle of lines and curves. He stared at the drawings, idly wondering if any might be worth saving.

Suddenly, he swore and leaned closer, studying the dozen or so rough sketches, noting the pattern that emerged.

And then he ripped off the sheet of paper, crumpled it viciously, and threw it across the room.

"You look like hell, Robeson. Must have been a long night." Antônio Rodríguez, one of the members of the board of directors gathered in Robeson and Company's executive meeting room, gave Alex a conspiratorial grin. "I hope it was worth it."

Another member of the board snorted with amusement. "With the women he dates, how could it *not* be worth it? And if it was the same woman he was with on Sugar Loaf," he added with a knowing smirk, "I think we can count ourselves fortunate that he showed up at all."

Several of the other men around the table laughed. Not a few of them looked a little envious.

Alex pointedly ignored them all.

"Your coffee, Mr. Robeson," said his secretary, setting a steaming cup beside his place at the table.

He gave a curt nod of thanks, but kept his attention on the stack of papers in front of him.

"I retrieved the item you wanted from the vault." Her voice was carefully expressionless. "It's in your desk, which I locked," she added, setting a key on the table beside the coffee cup.

Alex stared at the key, conscious of a painful churning in his belly that had nothing whatsoever to do with his having missed breakfast.

"Will that be all?" This time there was no mistaking the frost in her tone. Senhora Sanchez was not happy with him. Not happy at all.

He sucked in his breath, then slowly let it out. "Yes. Yes, thank you. That will be all."

Back straight, she spun around on her heel and strode from the room. The click of the latch as she shut the door behind her seemed almost unbearably loud, though no one else around the conference table seemed to notice.

Alex picked up the key and put it in the inner breast pocket of his suit jacket. He had a meeting to get through, he reminded himself. He wouldn't think about the jeweler's box that was now locked in his desk. Not yet.

In fact, he refused to think about it at all.

With a little more force than was really needed, he tapped the edge of his spoon against his water glass to silence the conversation around the table.

"The meeting will now come to order," he said. Distantly, he noted the stares of surprise at his harsh tone, but he cared no more for their opinion than he did Senhora Sanchez's. "I assume you've all had a chance to read the minutes of our last meeting?"

There was a general murmur of assent as heads nodded.

"If there are no changes, we'll go straight to the first order of business."

Papers rustled as the board of directors, with Alex at its head, got down to the business of the day.

Even though it had been late when Alex left and later still before she'd finally fallen asleep, Melisande was up at her usual early hour. The beach seemed whiter, the sky bluer, and the water more delightful than she ever remembered it, and as she jogged along the hard-packed sand at the water's edge she felt as though she might fly as easily as she danced through the bubbling white foam that licked at her toes each time a wave washed up.

When it was time to leave for the marina, she dressed with care, but paused often when the welling happiness within her threatened to burst out uncontrollably. She found herself suddenly singing snatches of songs, or giggling at nothing, and always there was a smile on her lips and a sparkle in her eyes.

The trim white slacks and brilliant turquoise top she finally chose only accented her glowing color and brought a jewel-like brilliance to her green eyes. Confident she looked her best and buoyed by a happy eagerness, Melisande felt capable of floating to the marina, but chose the more sedate transportation provided by a battered yellow taxi.

Her steps rang on the wooden planking of the pier as she walked past the long line of gracefully bobbing sailboats moored there. The brilliant sun reflected off the deep blue of the water and the glistening white of the boats, dazzling her. A soft breeze off the bay lifted the curls about her face, easing the humid heat of the Rio summer.

The Sebastians' boat was moored near the end. Despite the number of people about, laughingly preparing to enjoy the last, beautiful day of Carnaval, the Sebastians spotted her right away.

"Hello, Melisande," Maria shouted, waving enthusiastically. Even from a distance Melisande could see Stephen's broad smile of welcome.

Melisande's smile widened at the thought of having two such wonderful friends as the Sebastians. Her step quickened, and she soon found herself accepting Stephen's outstretched hand as he reached out to help her into the boat.

"You look wonderful," he exclaimed when she finally stood on the deck. "And I thought nothing could top Maria's good spirits today."

"Are you trying to make me jealous?" Maria demanded, laughing. She gave Melisande a quick hug. "Though you do look exceptionally well today. From the smile on your face, I'd guess you'd found the pot at the end of the rainbow or something."

"Or something," Melisande agreed, laughing with her lively friend. "What a wonderful day! You must have ordered it!"

"How'd you guess?"

"Intuition! Is Alex here yet?"

As she spoke his name, Melisande was aware that the Sebastians hadn't missed the eagerness in her voice or the increased glow of her smile, but she found she didn't care if such good friends shared in her happiness.

"Not yet. He said he'd be coming right after his meeting."

Maria cocked her head to the side, and her eyes were bright and inquisitive. She reminded Melisande of a lively, curious little red bird. "He also said he was taking you out to dinner the other night, after the ball. Did you have a nice time? Where did you go?"

"What is this, Maria? Twenty questions? Quit picking on poor Melisande. She just got here!"

Melisande couldn't help laughing at Stephen's defense of her, nor could she prevent the betraying blush that began to warm her cheeks.

"We had a *very* nice time. A really lovely time, in fact. He took me to The Inn."

"The Inn! But he never takes his girlfriends there. Never!" Maria was about to continue, but a sharp glance from her husband quelled the lively curiosity that threatened to start a torrent of questions and speculation. She subsided instead with a weak, "How nice."

It was clear, however, that nothing stopped her lively mind from considering the possibilities contained in Melisande's information.

"And then yesterday he helped me with some research in a private collection," Melisande added. She laughed. "He got rather cross about all the papers he had to read."

"Did he?" Maria said, fascinated.

Fortunately, at that moment Stephen glanced up and cried out, "Speak of the devil! You snuck up on us again, Alex. Melisande just got here, and we figured you wouldn't be far behind."

Suddenly shy, Melisande found herself backing against the opposite rail as Alex jumped onto the deck, staggering slightly as he landed without his usual grace.

He looked, she thought with a sudden, worried

frown, exhausted. It must have been a more important and difficult meeting than she'd thought, for
there was none of the usual vitality in his movements, and the dark circles under his eyes hadn't
been there the night before.

Love for him welled up within her. She longed
to go to him and rub the muscles of his shoulders,
which drooped with weariness. Instead, she stayed
against the rail, watching him greet their hosts.

It was a moment before she realized that both
Stephen and Maria looked oddly puzzled as they
studied the big man before them.

Stephen extended a hand to grip his friend's, but
his quietly spoken "Alex" sounded more like a
question than a greeting.

Maria stretched on tiptoe to brush Alex's cheek
with a friendly kiss, but withdrew quickly to stare
up into his face with puzzled uncertainty. "But,
Alex, what's the matter? What's happened?"

"I can't stay, Maria. I'm sorry." His words were
harsh and clipped and directed to the little redhead, but his eyes turned to Melisande.

He swallowed painfully, and a muscle in his jaw
twitched as though he were steeling himself to face
a formidable adversary.

As her eyes met his, the smile slowly left Melisande's face. She felt a cold, unreasoning dread
growing within her, forcing out the happiness that
had warmed her just a moment before.

Alex crossed to her, his steps heavy and graceless
on the gently moving deck. His eyes were black
holes in a face lined with fatigue. They held Melisande impaled, unable to look away.

"Alex? What is it? Is something wrong?"

He loomed over her, and as Melisande looked up into the dark depths of his eyes she almost cried out at the pain—and was it fear?—she saw in them. His jaw worked, and his lips quivered slightly as he fought to hold them clenched shut.

He said nothing for a long, long moment; then, as though it was wrenched from him against his will, he spoke her name with a groan that seemed to come from the depths of the agony that burned in his eyes. His hand came up in a gesture of supplication, then dropped; and he took an uncertain step back away from her.

"I brought you something." His voice was harsh, his breathing shallow and ragged. "I think it's best we not see each other. With our careers . . ."

He choked, then swallowed convulsively. Reaching into his pocket he pulled out a velvet-covered jeweler's box and held it out to her.

"Here. Take it. It's yours."

Melisande stared at the box that lay on his palm, and the blood drained from her face. The world seemed to wheel about her as some voice in her brain screamed an angry denial, but she couldn't move, couldn't lift her eyes from the velvet-covered box.

"Take it. It's for you."

He sounded angrier, but the words made no more sense the second time he spoke them. As though from a great distance, she heard someone, either Stephen or Maria, gasp in protest, but she could say nothing, do nothing.

A strong, dark hand reached out to grasp hers, forcing her fingers to close around the smooth velvet of the box. Slowly her gaze came up to meet his. She saw his pain, saw his upper lip twitch once before his mouth clamped shut in a harsh line.

Melisande's heartbeats thudded in her ears, pounding out an angry rhythm that warred with her uneven breathing. *This is reality,* she thought. *Not last night. That wasn't real. Not yesterday. Not Sugar Loaf.* This *is real. Horribly, painfully, inescapably real.*

Slowly she opened the box she held, then lifted out the golden bracelet that lay against the dark velvet.

As though she were another woman, totally unrelated to Melisande Merrick, she studied the heavy circle of gold that gleamed in the sunlight. Intricate ropes of gold twined around each other and the huge, square-cut, deep purple amethyst in the center of the band, irresistibly drawing the eye into the complex patterns that appeared and disappeared while she studied them. The central stone was magnificent, glowing with sudden flashes of pink and rose pink and lavender as the light touched its sparkling, perfectly cut facets.

It was one of the most beautiful pieces of jewelry she had ever seen. And it was hers. Identical bracelets belonged to other women Alex had known, then put aside.

Her mind continued to function, to analyze, as though fighting its way out of an obscuring mist, while the rest of her emotions remained frozen. Vaguely, she knew there was pain somewhere within her, but was unaware that it wouldn't touch her. Not yet.

Melisande heard Maria's cry of protest come from far away.

"No, Alex! You can't do that!"

But he had.

Melisande looked up. He hadn't moved in all that long, long time when she'd studied the bracelet she held. He seemed frozen in the same ice that held her pain trapped, safely distant, just as he was.

Her face calm, expressionless, Melisande extended the hand that held the bracelet out over the rail. Calmly, she studied the glinting gold and brilliant amethyst as they blazed in the sunlight.

Then, just as calmly, she dropped the band and watched it spin down into the crystal depths, glinting as it caught the light filtering through the blue until, with a last flash of gold, it disappeared into the darker waters below.

For a moment she watched the shifting waters in which the bracelet had disappeared; then she turned her attention back to the box she still held in her hands. Melisande closed it carefully, and extended it toward Alex.

"Here, Mr. Robeson," she said as he reached out numbly to take it from her. "I find I have no use for the bracelet, but I'm sure you'll be able to put the box to good use. Probably quite soon."

She took a deep breath, but her voice didn't change as she added, "I understand you go through quite a number of them."

Somewhere at the back of her mind she knew that she would always see the expression she now saw on his face. Perhaps someday she would have the courage to try to understand what it meant. But not now. Now she had to escape while her mind was still working and her pain was still frozen. The thaw was going to be terrible.

Turning from Alex, Melisande crossed the deck

to where Maria and Stephen stood. Their faces were twisted with sympathy for her and anger at the silent man behind her. Melisande knew that with her pain she would feel grief that these good, kind friends had had to be involved.

Now she simply said, "I'm sorry I've spoiled your last day of Carnaval. I know you will forgive me if I don't stay."

Without waiting for them to respond, she turned and climbed quickly onto the pier.

Behind her she heard an agonized cry of "Melisande!" She gave no sign that she'd heard, just walked away, her footsteps ringing on the wooden planking.

EIGHTEEN

"You should be quite pleased, Dr. Merrick. The company has decided to give a high priority to publishing your book. We're convinced it will be an even greater success than *The Famine*. Everyone who has read your manuscript is quite excited."

The little man behind the desk beamed with satisfaction as he contemplated the possible success of a book published by his company. Watching, Melisande expected him to rub his hands together and was vaguely disappointed when he didn't correspond to the stereotype she'd pictured.

"Of course I'm delighted, Mr. Sampson. I certainly never expected a book like this to attract much interest. *The Famine*, at least, dealt with a subject everyone knows something about."

Melisande leaned forward to pick up the revised pages that lay on the desk before her. There were so many memories tied up in the writing of them. By now she was accustomed to the familiar stab of pain they brought her and no longer had to fight the tears that had once threatened whenever she saw the book.

As she slowly turned the pages of the book—*her* book—she said, "I guess people are interested in it because it shows that human dreams and sufferings and hopes are universal."

She didn't mention "love," one of the words she'd used so often when talking to Alex about the women she was researching. She wondered if she would ever be able to use it again when she discussed the book.

Even after all these months she couldn't stop the twisting, tormenting pain her memories brought her, but she'd grown adept at hiding her feelings from the rest of the world.

If her friends questioned her on her unaccustomed, quiet sadness, or on the fact that she didn't eat as she should and had lost weight, or because she never laughed as she used to, she simply made excuses about the intense work on her book. Sometimes she wondered what she was going to use for an excuse now that the book was soon to be published and out of her hands, but that was definitely a case of "sufficient unto the day."

"The book is attracting attention because you have made the people you write about come alive," said Mr. Sampson, "made them live and breathe and hurt, just like people today. I couldn't put the book down, and my wife said the same thing."

Mr. Sampson, Melisande noted with amusement, really did rub his hands together in satisfaction.

She thought briefly of those long days and nights she'd spent working to finish the book. After that last time she'd seen Alex, she'd thrown herself into her work in a way she'd known to be destructive, but it was her only escape from the grinding pain that ate at her.

The book had consumed her. Once, she would

have delighted in the prospect of it becoming a success, reaching thousands of readers. Now, she was just glad it was done so that she could put it and the memories that were so closely tied to it out of her thoughts. She needed, desperately, to get on with her life . . . if only she could figure out how.

"Of course, I'm very grateful for all the support and enthusiasm, Mr. Sampson," she said now, calmly. "I certainly hope the book lives up to your expectations."

And that it's out of my life, she thought. The pain hadn't stopped as she'd hoped it would when she finished the book. Maybe, if she was lucky, it would stop once the book was published and completely out of her hands.

Mr. Sampson beamed. "I'm sure it will. And you may be sure that we are interested in publishing any future books you might write, Dr. Merrick."

Melisande saw the gleam in his eye and knew she should be pleased that there was already interest in her future books. But "future" was a word she couldn't think about now, hadn't been able to think about during the months that had passed since that last day of Carnaval in Rio.

Now she just wanted to get on with living. Her book was done, she didn't need to have that constant reminder of her foolishness before her anymore, and the future would just have to take care of itself.

Out on the street at last, she briefly considered flagging down a taxi, then decided on walking back to her apartment. It would be a long walk in the brisk, early spring air, but she needed the time and the anonymity of the crowded streets.

The past was past. Over and done with. She must remember that. When it occurred to her that Rio was warm and wonderful at this time of the year, she pushed that thought from her mind. When she found herself remembering dark eyes or the feel of gentle hands on her body, she forced those memories away as well.

Her refrain through these past long months had been the words she'd so happily quoted while she lay in Alex's arms, ". . . tomorrow, and tomorrow, and tomorrow."

He had been right to warn her against unhappy quotations. Away from fairyland, they were too apt a representation of reality.

The quote came from Shakespeare's *Macbeth*. "Tomorrow, and tomorrow, and tomorrow, Creeps in this petty pace from day to day, To the last syllable of recorded time . . ." The passage went on to speak of death and futility.

Too serious and too tragic for her own, too-common mistake of loving unwisely. But the rhythm of the words matched the beat of her steps on the sidewalk, and her days had moved in a petty pace that had dragged through the long hours of her work and the even longer hours of her solitary nights.

Once free of the book and the memories it inevitably stirred, it would be easier to forget. Though she wondered if she would ever completely do that. It didn't seem possible to love twice in one lifetime as she had loved Alex Robeson.

And always there was the small voice that said he had loved her, too, only his fear of the pain that rejection brought had led him to reject her as brutally as he had.

Small comfort. Whatever his feelings for her might have been, his rejection couldn't have been more cruel.

Despite her thoughts, the walk and brisk air had brought color back to her pale cheeks by the time she reached her apartment building, and Melisande entered the lobby with a quicker step than she had had for a long while.

She noticed the doorman wasn't at his usual place, but decided he must have been called away for some problem with another of the tenants. Melisande had made the down payment on her apartment with the first royalty check for *The Famine*. It seemed to her a secure refuge from the demanding outside world. She had furnished it with items she'd garnered from sales or junk stores, and the light yellows and greens she'd used to decorate brightened the rooms on even the darkest winter day. On such a gray day, she was looking forward to her new home's cozy cheeriness.

She would make herself some coffee, she decided in the elevator, and would settle in with the new murder mystery she'd bought the day before. No work and no memories.

Only after she'd crossed the landing from the elevator to her door did Melisande notice the tall man who had risen from one of the chairs in the little sitting area at the end of the corridor. A visitor for one of her neighbors, she thought, then froze.

Even with the intervening months, she couldn't mistake those broad shoulders or the powerful grace with which he moved.

Alex Robeson came out of the shadows of the sitting area toward her, and Melisande fought against a sudden, dizzying uncertainty, a desire to run, and an even stronger desire to be wrapped once again in those strong arms.

She watched him walk toward her, and a hundred thoughts whirled in her head, none of them intelligible. What should she say? What would he say? Should she shut the door of her apartment in his face or treat him with polite, but distant, courtesy? And why, oh why, was he here?

He stood beside her now, and it was too late to run, if that was what she ought to have done. Despite the months of pain and loneliness his rejection had caused, something within her was moved by the changes in him. He was thinner than he'd been, and though his shoulders were as broad as ever, his clothes no longer fit him with the smooth elegance of before. The lines and planes of his face were harder, sharper, and his eyes seemed to have receded until they looked out at her as though from a shadowed cave.

Whatever this man had done to her, she realized, he, too, had suffered. And she knew, with a certainty that recognized, then dismissed all her suffering, that she still loved him.

Alex started to speak, but stopped. A muscle jumped in his jaw, and he swallowed painfully. With an effort he said, "Hello, Melisande."

Her own voice was very soft, very calm. "Hello, Alex."

For a moment they stood silently, eyes locked in a wordless exchange that filled the space separating them with an electric tension. Then Melisande turned the key in the lock and opened the door to her apartment.

"I was just going to fix myself some coffee. Would you like some?"

He straightened and sighed, whether with relief or some other emotion, she couldn't tell.

"Thank you. I'd like that," he said, and stepped past her through the open door.

Turning to lock the door behind them, Melisande was threatened for a moment by the memory of Alex's closing the door to his apartment while she stood looking about her, waiting for him to come to her.

She resolutely pushed the memory down. She wouldn't let the past intrude more than it had to. Hadn't she been thinking about the need to live in the present, not the past and not the future, during her long walk home?

"Please, make yourself comfortable. May I take your coat? It won't take long to make the coffee, though I can't promise anything as good as what you can get in Rio."

Whatever Alex's reasons for coming to her, she was determined to maintain control over her own emotions, just as she had this morning in Mr. Sampson's office and as she had, at least in public, over the past months.

Wordlessly, Alex handed her the overcoat which had been slung over his arm when he'd come toward her in the hall outside. She felt his eyes follow her as she hung their coats in the small closet near the door. Though she deliberately kept her attention on the simple task of putting away the coats, she sensed that he was both grateful for her calm politeness and confused by it.

Without glancing at him again, she went into the kitchen, glad to have a moment to gather her thoughts and control the emotions raging within her. It was one thing to tell herself that she was going to maintain a calm demeanor, another thing to actually maintain it when just being near him was arousing feelings she'd thought had died after all the pain he'd caused her.

When she at last reappeared bearing a tray loaded with all the necessities for coffee for two, she found him standing before the floor-to-ceiling bookcases that filled two walls of the living room. He returned the book he was holding to its place on the crowded shelves and came to take the tray from her hands.

"Is the coffee table all right?" he asked. At her nod of assent, he carefully placed the tray on top of several large art books, then tentatively settled himself in a comfortable armchair.

Melisande chose a seat on the sofa across from him, but found she couldn't meet his eyes. She bent to fill a cup from the pottery coffeepot.

"You prefer your coffee black, don't you?" she asked, and was suddenly overcome by the simple intimacy her question implied.

"Yes, thank you."

The voice is the same, she thought. She'd even heard it in her dreams. The hand he stretched out to take the cup and saucer from her was the same. She couldn't raise her eyes to meet his, but the sight of those long, elegant fingers as they came so close to hers without ever touching her was as unsettling as a caress.

Without glancing at him, she poured a cup of coffee for herself, grateful that the act of stirring in the sugar could occupy her attention for another few seconds.

"You have a lovely home, Melisande. It seems so like you, warm and feminine and wel—" He broke off, then added—"so bright."

Had he been about to say "welcoming"? Melisande wondered. Did it seem so for him?

And, more important, what had prompted her to let him into her sanctuary?

She suddenly wanted to scream away the tension growing within her. *Why did you come here? How could you have hurt me like that? Why can't you just take me in your arms and kiss away these last few months? Didn't you know I loved you?*

"Thank you," was all she said, very quietly.

She couldn't avoid looking at him any longer. With deliberate calm, she brought her gaze up to meet his. For a long moment the silence between them was an almost palpable thing.

Her impression in the hall had been accurate— he *had* lost weight. The drawn lines about his eyes stood out clearly, there was a haunted look in those dark eyes, and the uncertainty in his bearing hadn't been there before.

She'd learned enough of suffering to recognize it in another, especially in a man whom she couldn't help loving. Her anger at the pain he'd inflicted was as nothing beside the love that came welling up within her now.

"Oh, Alex, what have you done to us?" she asked softly, a catch in her throat. "To both of us?"

For a long moment, he didn't move, but his nostrils flared with his effort to control his unsteady breathing; then he reached out to return his cup to the tray. His fingers trembled, making the china clink, ever so faintly.

Abruptly, he lunged out of the chair and turned to pace the room with an unsteady, jerky stride. He ran a hand through his hair in a nervous gesture Melisande had never seen him use before, until his thick, black hair was completely disheveled.

She watched him and fought against a wild hope that there might be such a thing as a happy ending after all. It was foolish to let a hope like that exist. She had suffered enough—too much.

Yet even as she thought it, a dangerous little voice inside her whispered, *so has he.*

Just as abruptly as he'd begun, Alex stopped his pacing and came to stand over her. He panted with the violence of the emotion that drove him, and his eyes stared wildly from their shadowed sockets.

"How can you *be* like that? After what I did to you, how can you just invite me in for a cup of coffee and ask me a question like that?"

Rough hands jerked Melisande to her feet. She grabbed his arms to steady herself and found her face only inches from his own convulsed features. She felt her pulse pounding through her veins and knew a wild, exultant joy that came with the power love imparted.

He loved her. He loved her as much as she loved him.

Gently, she touched his cheek in a gesture of benediction and forgiveness.

"I can because I love you, Alex Robeson."

Roughly, he thrust her to arm's length without ever releasing his hold of her. He shook her, once. "How can you? After what I did? Are you crazy?"

She laughed, the first real laugh she'd known in months. "I do. And yes, I think I am."

"What?" he demanded, clearly confused.

"I love you, Alex Robeson," she said, cupping his face in her hands, drawing him down to her. "And, yes, I think I am just a little crazy. But that's all right, isn't it? Now?"

For a long moment he stared at her as if demented, then, with a groan that was almost a sob, he pulled her into his arms and his lips came down to meet hers in a violent kiss that carried with it all the pain that was between them—and all the love that would wash the pain away.

Eventually, Melisande found herself beside him on the sofa, clinging to him, her face, wet with happy tears, pressed against the fine cloth of his suit, his arms wrapped about her in a protective embrace that couldn't disguise the trembling of his body against hers.

His voice trembled, as well. "Oh, God, Melisande. I couldn't stay away any longer, but I was so afraid . . . I didn't dare to hope, yet I had to come. I *had* to."

"I thought I'd never see you again. I thought I didn't want to." Melisande fought to control the quaver in her own voice. "Then I saw you coming toward me, and I thought . . . I don't know what I thought. But it doesn't matter. Do we have to think?"

He didn't answer, and Melisande felt him grow tense against her. She pulled away from him enough to look into his eyes, so close above hers.

"Alex, what's wrong?"

There was determination in the dark eyes that met hers. Firmly, he put her from him without taking his eyes from her. She saw his jaws clench.

"I have to say this, Melisande, while I have the courage. I've been cursing myself for a frightened fool ever since I drove you from me. I've been in New York for almost a month. Every day I've come to this building, and every day I've run away because I couldn't bear to have you refuse to see me as you had every right to do."

He ran a trembling hand through his hair. "I was just about to run away again when you stepped off that elevator."

Melisande repressed an urge to comfort him. Let him speak. Let him get all the ugly words out in the open. They needed the truth—for both their sakes.

"That night, after we . . ."—Alex gulped, then continued—"after we made love, I went home and all I could think of was you, how you felt in my arms, how your eyes lighted up when you laughed. I could smell your perfume on my skin, I swear I could *feel* you, and I wanted you there so badly I ached."

He reached out to clasp her hand. "I don't know when I fell in love with you, but I guess I'd been doing it all along. You were always so proud, yet gentle. Everyone liked and admired you. I would watch the way you were with people and how they responded to you, how serious you were about your work."

Melisande still said nothing, but she felt a surge of happiness wash through her. She'd been so sure, there in Rio, that he *had* cared for her, at least a little. In spite of what he'd done, that thought had been a comfort through the long months since. It was good to know she hadn't been wrong.

"I only realized how I felt about you that last night, and then I went crazy. When I left you at your apartment and came home, I was floating. Everywhere I went in the apartment I saw you. I couldn't work. I couldn't sleep."

He stopped, and his tongue licked lips suddenly gone dry. "Ever since I was a kid," he said at last, hesitantly, "I've worked with jewelry."

Melisande frowned, puzzled by his change of subject.

"My father insisted I learn to make it. He said it would help me understand the business better. It was a surprise to everyone when it turned out I have a talent for that sort of thing. I like it, and I find it's soothing. Sometimes, when I can't focus on my work, can't sleep, I'll work on designs." He drew in a shaky breath. "But you know all that, don't you?"

The pause in his narration lengthened until Melisande said gently, "Go on."

Their eyes met, but Alex's dropped first.

He continued, "I sat down that night intending to work, but instead I started sketching, trying to get my mind off you. It was a while before I realized that I was sketching rings." His eyes came back up to meet hers. "Wedding rings."

Alex ignored Melisande's sudden gasp of surprise and rushed on.

"That's when I went crazy. I panicked. I'd sworn years ago that I'd never be trapped into marriage. I thought I'd learned that most women *I* knew only wanted money and expensive things and didn't give a damn about *me*."

He drew a deep breath, then continued. "Maria told me later, after you left Rio, that you knew about those damnable bracelets. She said I'd lost the best chance at happiness I'd ever have. I already knew that by then. I realized it the moment I saw your face when I handed you that jeweler's box, knew it long before you dumped that damned bracelet in the harbor."

Alex turned to her, his eyes glowing. Gently he leaned to brush a kiss across her parted lips, then took her head between his hands and smiled down into her upturned face.

"I was so proud of you. Even through the crazy fear of loving you, I was proud." A shadow passed across his features, and his hands fell from her face. "But by then it was too late. I let you walk off that boat, and I never went after you, never tried to beg your forgiveness."

"You know," Melisande said softly, "I don't think it would have made any difference. At least at first. You hurt me so, I don't think I would have listened to anything you would have said."

She hesitated, searching for the words she wanted. "Alex, today I walked back from my publisher's, and I had time for a lot of thinking. These past months have been hell for me, but today I knew I had to begin to live in the present, not in the past."

She laid her open palm comfortingly against his cheek. "You've been living in the past, and it nearly destroyed both of us."

Alex cupped his hand over hers, then turned his head to place a gentle kiss in her palm.

"That's what I've learned by loving you," he said softly. "But it's not that easy. My life since you left has been hell, but it's a hell of my own making. I don't know how good I am at living just in the present."

"Let's try it for just a little while, Alex," Melisande whispered. "Until we both learn how. Then maybe we can begin to think about a future."

For a joyous moment Melisande thought she might drown in the love she saw shining in his face, but before she could move into his arms he sat back from her, frowning.

Slowly, he reached into his pocket and pulled out a soft suede pouch, thoughtfully weighing it in his hand a moment before abruptly forcing it into Melisande's.

"Alex?" Fright suddenly made her voice tremble.

"Open the pouch. Please, Melisande. I've spent all these months working on it. It was the only thing that kept me going."

Hesitantly, she fumbled with the silken cords that tied the pouch, but when she finally succeeded in unfastening them, she paused, uncertain.

She glanced up to find Alex watching her nervously. Yet, beyond his nervousness, she could see only love. It was all the reassurance she needed.

With deliberate care, she lifted the pouch and shook its contents into her open hand.

There were two rings, but they seemed one, so closely were their settings intertwined. Twisted gold leaves set with flawless white diamonds on one ring wrapped around the single gem of the second ring, a large, heart-shaped emerald of the deepest, clearest green Melisande had ever seen.

"You can toss these, too, if you want, Melisande. I'll understand."

When she simply stared at them, not speaking, he took the rings from her and carefully separated them. Retaining the emerald, he held out the ring with diamonds to her.

"They say that diamonds are forever, but I'd like them to be for today, for right now." Alex's voice was low but his eyes burned with his love for her. "For our present, Melisande, our today."

Her voice was very soft, almost trembling, as she said, "And the emerald?"

"A pledge for the future. A future we can share if you'll trust me enough to let me build one for both of us."

Tears stung her eyes, but they were tears of joy to wash away the bitter tears of pain.

"I do," she said, smiling through her tears. "I will."

She had no time to say more before Alex, with a choked cry of joy, drew her to him and wrapped her in an embrace that shut out the past forever.

BOOK YOUR PLACE ON OUR WEBSITE AND MAKE THE READING CONNECTION!

We've created a customized website just for our very special readers, where you can get the inside scoop on everything that's going on with Zebra, Pinnacle and Kensington books.

When you come online, you'll have the exciting opportunity to:

- View covers of upcoming books

- Read sample chapters

- Learn about our future publishing schedule (listed by publication month *and author*)

- Find out when your favorite authors will be visiting a city near you

- Search for and order backlist books from our online catalog

- Check out author bios and background information

- Send e-mail to your favorite authors

- Meet the Kensington staff online

- Join us in weekly chats with authors, readers and other guests

- Get writing guidelines

- AND MUCH MORE!

Visit our website at
http://www.zebrabooks.com

Coming September 1999 From Bouquet Romances

#9 If You Loved Me by Vanessa Grant
__(0-8217-6313-X, $3.99) When her son disappeared on a kayaking trip, Seattle Surgeon Emma Garrett needed the help of wilderness expert Gary Mckenzie . . . her first and greatest love. Even after years apart they were still drawn together by the passion they once shared. But is it enough to find Emma's son and build a life together?

#10 Caitlyn's Cowboy by Gina Jackson
__(0-8217-66314-8, $3.99) Boston Socialite Caitlyn Bradford was starting a new life in Wyoming when she discovered she inherited half a ranch . . . and a partner. Dane Morrison was pure cowboy and not looking for love, but he couldn't help being captivated by the beautiful, sophisticated city gal.

#11 Mountain Magic by Susan Hardy
__(0-8217-6315-6, $3.99) Clementine Harper loved roaming the woods of her beloved North Carolina mountains searching for gems to design her jewelry with. Unfortunately, her lifestyle was threatened by New York banker, Will Fletcher, who accused her of trespassing on his land. But with a woman as charming as Clem, Will found it hard not to be pulled into her mountain magic.

#12 All in the Family by Judy Gill
__(0-8217-6316-4, $3.99) Divorced dad Jed Cotts was fed up with his daughters' attempts to fix him up, until he found himself going away for the weekend with lovely Karen Anderson. Could he let himself fall in love again? How could he not?

Call toll free **1-888-345-BOOK** to order by phone or use this coupon to order by mail.

Name _____

Address_____

City _____ State _____ Zip _____

Please send me the books I have checked above.

I am enclosing $_____

Plus postage and handling* $_____

Sales tax (where applicable) $_____

Total amount enclosed $_____

*Add $2.50 for the first book and $.50 for each additional book.
Send check or Money order (no cash or CODs) to:
Kensington Publishing Corp., 850 Third Avenue,
New York, NY 10022
Prices and Numbers subject to change without notice. Valid only in the U.S.
Books will be available 8/1/99. All orders subject to availability.
Check out our web site at **www.kensingtonbooks.com**

Put a Little Romance in Your Life With
Fern Michaels

__Dear Emily	0-8217-5676-1	$6.99US/$8.50CAN
__Sara's Song	0-8217-5856-X	$6.99US/$8.50CAN
__Wish List	0-8217-5228-6	$6.99US/$7.99CAN
__Vegas Rich	0-8217-5594-3	$6.99US/$8.50CAN
__Vegas Heat	0-8217-5758-X	$6.99US/$8.50CAN
__Vegas Sunrise	1-55817-5983-3	$6.99US/$8.50CAN
__Whitefire	0-8217-5638-9	$6.99US/$8.50CAN